CHILDRᴇ
ENCYCLOPᴇᴅɪᴀ
THE WORLD OF KNOWLEDGE

SCIENTISTS, INVENTIONS
And
DISCOVERIES

by

Manasvi Vohra

V&S PUBLISHERS

Published by:

V&S PUBLISHERS

F-2/16, Ansari road, Daryaganj, New Delhi-110002
☎ 23240026, 23240027 • *Fax:* 011-23240028
✉ info@vspublishers.com • ⊕ www.vspublishers.com

Online Brandstore: amazon.in/vspublishers

Regional Office : Hyderabad
5-1-707/1, Brij Bhawan (Beside Central Bank of India Lane)
Bank Street, Koti, Hyderabad - 500 095
☎ 040-24737290
✉ vspublishershyd@gmail.com

Follow us on:

BUY OUR BOOKS FROM: AMAZON FLIPKART

DISCLAIMER

While every attempt has been made to provide accurate and timely information in this book, neither the author nor the publisher assumes any responsibility for errors, unintended omissions or commissions detected therein. The author and publisher makes no representation or warranty with respect to the comprehensiveness or completeness of the contents provided.

All matters included have been simplified under professional guidance for general information only, without any warranty for applicability on an individual. Any mention of an organization or a website in the book, by way of citation or as a source of additional information, doesn't imply the endorsement of the content either by the author or the publisher. It is possible that websites cited may have changed or removed between the time of editing and publishing the book.

Results from using the expert opinion in this book will be totally dependent on individual circumstances and factors beyond the control of the author and the publisher.

It makes sense to elicit advice from well informed sources before implementing the ideas given in the book. The reader assumes full responsibility for the consequences arising out from reading this book.

For proper guidance, it is advisable to read the book under the watchful eyes of parents/guardian. The buyer of this book assumes all responsibility for the use of given materials and information.

The copyright of the entire content of this book rests with the author/publisher. Any infringement/transmission of the cover design, text or illustrations, in any form, by any means, by any entity will invite legal action and be responsible for consequences thereon.

Printed at : Param Offsetters, Okhla, New Delhi–110020

PUBLISHER'S NOTE

V&S Publishers — Leading Publisher of Children and Academic Books in India for over a decade, is glad to announce the launch of a unique, fully *coloured set of five books* under the head, *Children's Encyclopedia – The World of Knowledge.* The set of 5 books namely – *Life Sciences and the Human Body, Physics and Chemistry, Space Science and Electronics, Scientists and Inventions* and *General Knowledge* has been especially developed keeping in mind the students and children of all age groups, particularly from 6 to 14 years of age. Our main aim is to arouse interest and solve the queries of school children regarding various and diverse topics of Science and help them master the subject thoroughly. After the resounding success of 71 Science Trailblazing Series, we present you with this new arrival of ours.

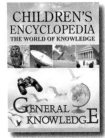 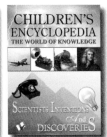 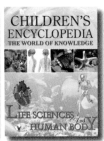 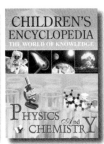 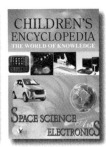

In the book, *Scientists, Inventions and Discoveries*, in the first part (Par-I) the author has broadly dealt with some world renowned and famous Scientists such as *Archimedes, Alexander Graham Bell, Albert Einstein, Benjamin Franklin, Charles Robert Darwin, Galileo Galilei, George Eastman, Sir Isaac Newton, Louis Pasteur, Michael Faraday, Marie Curie,* etc. The second part (Part-II), on the other hand, focusses mainly on their popular Inventions & Discoveries like *Bacteria, Vitamins, Rabies Vaccine, Penicillin, Aeroplane, Electricity, Cinema, Electric Bulb,* and so on...

Each chapter is followed by a section called **Quick Facts** that contains a set of interesting and fascinating facts about the topics already discussed in the chapter. There are also **Exercises** compiled at the end of the book followed by a **Glossary** of difficult words and scientific terms to make the book complete and comprehensive.

Though our aim is to be flawless, but errors might have crept in inadvertently. So we request our esteemed readers to read the book thoroughly and offer valuable suggestions wherever necessary to improve and enhance the quality of the book. Hope it interests you all and serves its purpose well.

CONTENTS

PART-I SCIENTISTS

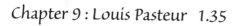

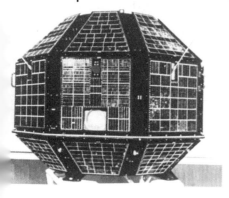

PART-II
INVENTIONS &
DISCOVERIES

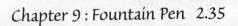

SCIENTISTS

SCIENTISTS

Chapter - 1

ARCHIMEDES
(287 BC–212 BC)

Biography

Archimedes was a Greek mathematician, physicist, astronomer, engineer and inventor. He is famous for giving what is today known as 'Archimedes Principle' among his other works. He was also famous for Archimedes' screw, hydrostatics, levers and infinitesimals.

Archimedes

Archimedes was born in the ancient city of Syracuse, Sicily in C 287 BC.

Did You Know?

Archimedes was asked by *King Hieron II* to test a gold crown of its purity without melting the crown. Archimedes was getting into his bathtub thinking over the question when he noticed the water level rising. He ran out crying 'Eureka' on the streets but without his clothes!

Archimedes Principle

Archimedes stated that whenever a solid object is wholly or partially immersed in water, it experiences an upward force by water. This force is called the 'Buoyant' force which displaces certain amount of water. The amount of the water displaced is equal to the volume of that object.

You must have seen very heavy logs of wood floating through rivers or boats and ships moving on water. Logs of wood float on water because of the Archimedes Principle of buoyancy. Same is the case with boats and ships. A boat keeps floating because water gives it an upward push. The heavier the load gets on the boat, the water pushes it upward with more force. But if the water comes up to the level of the boat's edge, there would be no more upward push and the boat will sink.

Archimedes has many inventions and discoveries to his credit. He contributed in the field of *mathematics, science and defence*. Following are some of his works:

- 💣 **Archimedes Screw:** This was used to lift water from a low-lying water body to a certain height.

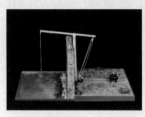
Archimedes Screw

- 💣 **Claw of Archimedes:** The Claw of Archimedes is a weapon that he is said to have designed in order to defend the city of Syracuse. Also known as "the ship shaker," the claw consisted of a crane-like arm from which a large metal grappling hook was suspended. When the claw was dropped onto an attacking ship, the arm would swing upwards, lifting the ship out of the water and possibly sinking it. There have been modern experiments to test the feasibility of the claw, and in 2005, a television documentary entitled Superweapons of the

Archimedes Claw

Ancient World built a version of the claw and concluded that it was a workable device.

- 💣 **Value of Pie:** It is a very significant discovery in the field of Mathematics. Archimedes showed that the value of pi (π) is greater than 223/71 and less than **22/7**. The latter figure was used as an approximation of pi throughout the Middle Ages and is still used today when only a rough figure is required.

- 💣 **On the Equilibrium of Planes (two volumes):** The first book is in 15 propositions with seven postulates, while the second book is in ten propositions. In this work, Archimedes explained the Law of the Lever, stating, "Magnitudes are in equilibrium at distances reciprocally proportional to their weights." Archimedes uses the principles derived to calculate the areas and centres of gravity of various geometric figures including *triangles, parallelograms and parabolas*.

- 💣 **Archimedes Heat Rays:** Mirrors were placed at different angles on seashores so that all of them reflect the sunrays at a single point, usually on an enemy ship during the war. The amount of sun's heat would be so high that it would burn the ship.

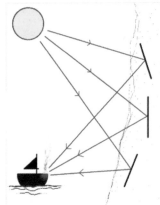

Archimedes Heat Rays

✻   Archimedes was able to use infinitesimals in a way that is similar to the modern integral calculus. This technique is known as the method of exhaustion, and he employed it to the approximate the value of π which is approximately **3.1416**. He also proved that the area of a circle was equal to π multiplied by the square of the radius of the circle (πr^2).

On the Sphere and Cylinder, Archimedes postulates that any magnitude when added to itself enough times will exceed any given magnitude. This is the Archimedean property of real numbers.

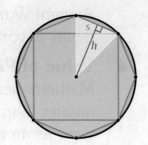

Archimedes was killed by the Roman soldiers when collaborators let the Romans into Syracuse in 212 BC.

Quick Facts

- Archimedes was one of the greatest scientists who created the science of mechanics and hydrostatics.

- Archimedes was a Greek who lived in the city of Syracuse, Sicily. His relative, Hieron II, was the king of Syracuse.

- To help defend Syracuse against Roman attackers in 215BC, Archimedes invented many war machines. They included an awesome 'claw' — a giant grappling crane that could lift whole galleys from the water and sink them.

- He stated that the volume of an object is the amount of surface occupied by it. He also discovered that objects float because they are thrust upwards by the water.

- Archimedes analysed levers mathematically. He showed that the load you can move with a particular effort is in exact proportion to its distance from the fulcrum.

Chapter - 2

ALEXANDER GRAHAM BELL
(1847–1922)

Alexander Graham Bell is one of the pioneering inventors of the modern age. Born in *Edinburgh, Scotland* on March 3, 1847, Bell was a scientist, inventor, engineer and innovator. He invented the first **'Telephone'**.

Alexander Graham Bell

Biography

Alexander went to the *University of Edinburgh* and later to the *University of London*. Bell was a remarkable child and at a very young age of 12, he made his first invention – a wheat dehusking machine fitted with a set of paddles and nail brushes.

Discoveries and Inventions

Since a very young age, he was involved in devising ways to help the deaf-mute people communicate. He devised hearing instruments for the deaf people and based on these, he progressed to the invention of telephone. *He established a school*

A Wheat Husking Machine

for the deaf and mutes in Boston, Massachusetts in 1872. He made his first telephone on June 2, 1875 and at the age of 29, Bell presented his first 'telephone' to the world in the year 1876. In 1877, he formed the Bell Telephone Company.

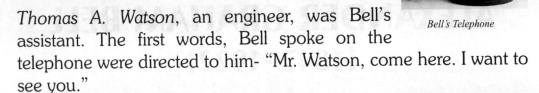

Bell's Telephone

Did You Know?

Thomas A. Watson, an engineer, was Bell's assistant. The first words, Bell spoke on the telephone were directed to him- "Mr. Watson, come here. I want to see you."

After the invention of telephone, Bell invented a 'photophone' – a device that enabled sound to be transmitted through a beam of light. This device was made from a sensitive selenium crystal and a mirror that vibrated in response to a sound. Bell regarded this invention as his greatest, even greater than the telephone. Today's fibre, laser and optics communication systems are based on the *principles of Alexander Graham Bell's photophone.*

Bell was engaged in a wide variety of scientific researches and inventions like aeroplanes, telecommunication, artificial respiration, etc.

Bell's Photophone

Bell is also credited with the invention of the metal detector in 1881. The device was quickly put together in an attempt to find the bullet in the body of US President James Garfield. The metal detector worked flawlessly in tests but did not find the assassin's bullet partly because the metal bed frame on which the President was lying disturbed the instrument, resulting in static.

In 1891, Bell had begun experiments to develop the motor-powered heavier-than-air, aircraft. The AEA was first formed as Bell shared

the vision to fly with his wife, who advised him to seek "young" help as Alexander was 60 years old.

In 1898, Bell experimented with tetrahedral box kites, with wings constructed of multiple compound tetrahedral kites covered in maroon silk. The tetrahedral wings were named Cygnet I, II and III, and were flown both

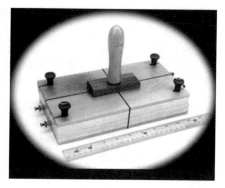
Bell's Metal Detector

unmanned and manned (Cygnet I crashed during a flight carrying Selfridge) in the period from 1907–1912. Some of Bell's kites are on display at the Alexander Graham Bell National Historic Site.

Alexander Graham Bell died on August 2, 1922 due to diabetic complications.

Quick Facts

- Alexander Graham Bell's first vocation was that of a teacher of the Deaf. Not only did Bell follow in his father's footsteps (the elder Bell's work in Visible Speech for the Deaf inspired Shaw's Pygmalion), but Bell's mother and wife were also deaf!

- Graham Bell's two brothers, Melville and Edward died at a very young age of the deadly disease, Tuberculosis.

- Alexander Graham Bell was an American inventor but a Scottish by birth.

- In the United States he began teaching the deaf-mutes, publicising the system called visible speech. He also became a naturalised U.S. citizen in 1882.

- In 1880, France bestowed on Bell the Volta Prize, worth 50,000 francs, for his remarkable invention of the Telephone. He used the money in founding the Volta Laboratory in Washington, D.C. and invented the photophone with his associates.

- Bell's other inventions include the audiometer, the induction balance, and the first wax recording cylinder, introduced in 1886.

- Bell was one of the co-founders of the National Geographic Society, and he served as its president from 1896 to 1904.

- He also helped to establish the journal, Science by financing it from 1883-1894.

Chapter - 3

ALBERT EINSTEIN
(1879–1955)

Albert Einstein is one of the best known scientists of modern age. A *German* by origin, Einstein was born on March 14, 1879. He is famous for his *'Theory of Relativity'* giving the very famous equation $E = mc^2$. He was conferred the **Nobel Prize** for his contribution in the field of Physics. He is said to be the **Father of Modern Physics**.

Albert Einstein

Biography

Albert Einstein was born at *Ulm, in Württemberg, Germany*. He did his basic schooling from Luitpold Gymnasium, Munich. Einstein obtained his doctor's degree in 1905 and in 1914, and was appointed as a Professor of the University of Berlin. He received a *Nobel Prize* in Physics in the year, 1921. In 1933, Einstein migrated to America as a Professor of Theoretical Physics at Princeton and became a US citizen in 1940.

Did You Know?

Einstein once remarked, "A question that sometimes drives me crazy: am I or the others are crazy?"

Discoveries and Inventions

Albert Einstein's most salient work, for which he is justly famous for, is the Theory of relativity which was published in 1916. It states that the energy possessed by an object depends upon the mass of that object.

$E = mc^2$ where, E = energy, m = mass of the object, c = the speed of light

The more the mass of the object, the more the amount of energy it has.

He also worked to shed light on many areas of Physics and found the basis of some important revelations on which works like *Quantum Physics, Photoelectric Effect and Brownian Motion* are based.

Some of Einstein's important and well-known scholarly works are the *Special Theory of Relativity* (1905), *Relativity* (English translations, 1920 and 1950), *General Theory of Relativity* (1916), *Investigations on the Theory of Brownian Movement* (1926), and *The Evolution of Physics* (1938).

About Zionism (1930), *Why War?* (1933), *My Philosophy* (1934), and *Out of My Later Years* (1950) are perhaps some of his most popular non-scientific works.

Einstein died on April 18, 1955 due to internal bleeding. He worked until the very end of his life, such was his genius.

Quick Facts

- Einstein was actually born with an abnormally large head which doctors were concerned could be a sign that he was mentally retarded.

- He was later awarded the Nobel Prize for his work on the photo-electric effect.

- In 1895, at the age of 17, Albert Einstein applied for early admission into the Swiss Federal Polytechnical School (Eidgenössische Technische Hochschule or ETH). He passed the math and science sections of the entrance exam, but failed the rest, i.e., (history, languages, geography, etc.)!

Chapter - 4

BENJAMIN FRANKLIN
(1706–1790)

Benjamin Franklin was a celebrated American scientist, politician and author. He is regarded as one of the founding fathers of the United States. He was also the first United States Ambassador to France.

Biography

Benjamin Franklin was born on January 17, 1706 in Boston, Massachusetts. He did his schooling from Boston Latin School. Benjamin started working in his brother's newspaper as an apprentice. Later on in his life, he proved to be a successful newspaper editor and printer. He was the first to build a public library in America and a fire station in Pennsylvania. Benjamin ventured in many businesses, but is remembered mainly as a scientist.

Benjamin Franklin

Did You Know?

Benjamin Franklin never got a patent against his inventions as he believed that his work is for public welfare and not to gain profit.

Discoveries and Inventions

Franklin has many discoveries and inventions to his credit. He discovered the 'principle of conservation of energy'. After his famous experiment with an iron key attached to a kite, he concluded that buildings could be saved from striking lightning (electric charge from the clouds) by placing a sharp pointed iron rod on the topmost part of the building, which goes all the way under the earth. This way, the electric charge would pass through the rod to the earth without affecting the building. He invented the 'lightning rod' for this purpose, which are used all over the world now. He was the one to name opposite charges of electricity as 'positive' and 'negative'.

Did You Know?

Benjamin Franklin *invented a tool*-long arm – a wooden rod with a clawing hand to reach to the books kept on high shelves.

Franklin also gave the world, *'bifocals'* – spectacles with two lenses in each frame so that a person could use the same spectacle for watching near and far things at the same time. Among his other inventions are Franklin stove, glass armonica and odometer.

Benjamin Franklin died on April 17, 1790 in Philadelphia.

Quick Facts

- Benjamin Franklin was the ninth child out of eleven children. His father was Josiah a candle/soap maker.

- When he was 16, he became a vegetarian so he could spend his money on books instead of meat. He was the first mailman in Philadelphia.

- He was a civil worker, inventor, a founding father, scientist, publisher and author, and held many political positions such as Minister to France which caused frequent travel to other countries.

- He was the only person to sign the Constitution, Declaration of Independence, and the Treaty of Paris of 1776.

- Benjamin Franklin was at the age of seventy when he signed the Declaration of Independence.

Chapter - 5

CHARLES ROBERT DARWIN
(1809–1882)

Charles Robert Darwin was an *English scientist and naturalist.* He is famously remembered for his scientific theory of evolution named as *'Natural Selection'.*

Biography

Charles Robert Darwin was born on February 12, 1809 in Shrewsbury, Shorpshire, England in a wealthy family. He was the fifth child. Darwin graduated from the elite school of Shrewsbury in 1825. After that, he enrolled in the University of Edinburgh to study medicine. But in 1827, he dropped out of Edinburgh and got admitted to the University of Cambridge. On completing his graduation in 1831, a 22-year-old Darwin embarked on a journey of scientific exploration as a naturalist around the world.

Charles Robert Darwin

Discoveries and Inventions

After returning back from his expedition in 1836, Darwin started recording his views and ideas on the evolution process of the earth, based on the things he had observed during his voyage. By 1838, he had a rough sketch of his theory of evolution through natural selection. This theory was first announced in 1858.

The Theory of Evolution through Natural Selection states that an individual born in any species has to compete with its surrounding

Evolution of Man

for its survival. The cycle goes on like this and that particular species evolve along with some variations depending upon its surroundings. These variations are passed on to the next generation through heredity, thus marking the evolution of the species.

Did You Know?

The Theory of Evolution through Natural Selection gave the phrase, 'Survival of the fittest'.

Darwin observed that all related organisms are evolved from common ancestors. He also mentioned that the earth is an evolving entity and not static in nature.

Darwin's Theory of Evolution met with criticism from his fraternity. Fellow scientists criticised him saying that he can't prove his theory. Others challenged him to prove his theory of origin of variation in species and how it is possible to pass those variations to the next generation.

Charles Robert Darwin died on April 19, 1882 in his home near London.

Quick Facts

🗣 February 12, 1809, was a very significant day in history. Not only was Charles Darwin born that day, the famous President of the United States, Abraham Lincoln was also born that day.

🗣 Charles Darwin is often called the "Father of Evolution".

🗣 Darwin attended the Edinburgh University in a hope of becoming a physician like his father, but soon abandoned the idea because he couldn't stand the sight of blood.

🗣 Charles Darwin was quite sick in his later years. He is believed to have caught Chagas Disease while in South America. This disease is caused by the bite of a certain bug.

🗣 Even though Charles Darwin was not a Buddhist himself, he and his wife Emma had an alleged fascination of and respect for the religion. Darwin wrote a book called Expressions of the Emotions in Man and Animals in which he explained that compassion in humans was a trait that survived natural selection because it is a beneficial trait to want and stop the suffering of others.

Chapter - 6

GALILEO GALILEI
(1564–1642)

Galileo was an Italian mathematician, astronomer, physicist and philosopher. He is famously remembered for the Galilean Telescope and his observations of the universe.

Biography

Galileo was born on February 15, 1564 in Pisa, Italy. His father was a musician and wool trader. He wanted his son to study medicine. Galileo began his education in Jesuit monastery at the age of 11. By the time he was 17, he was enrolled with the University of Pisa to learn medicine.

Galileo Galilei

In university, mathematics became his favourite subject, so much so that he shunned other subjects and began studying only maths. Later, to earn his living, he began taking maths tuitions for other students.

Did You Know?

Galileo wanted to be a monk when he came back from the Jesuit monastery. His father got angry and withdrew him from there.

Discoveries and Inventions

At the age of 21, he discovered the 'law of pendulum'. He saw a lamp swing to and fro from the ceiling of a church. He then timed the swinging of the lamp with his pulse and to his astonishment, found that each swing was completed in equal time. This formed the basis of the law of pendulum. He invented the military compass.

But his most important invention was the Galilean telescope. He started with a 3-power telescope and later refined it to 10- power. It was through this telescope that he noticed that the moon has craters and that planets revolve around the sun. This observation made him support the heliocentric theory stated by **Nicolaus Copernicus**. *This theory states that the Sun is a stationary star and is at the centre of the Solar System. The Earth revolves around it and not the other way round.*

Galileo also challenged Aristotle's theory which states heavy objects fall at a greater speed during a free fall. Galileo dropped balls of different masses and sizes at the same time from the top of the Tower

Galilean Telescope

of Pisa. All the balls hit the ground at the same time. Galileo then stated that time taken by a free falling object to reach the ground is independent of its mass.

Galileo Galilei died on March 8, 1642 following a prolonged illness.

Quick Facts

- Galileo Galilei taught geometry, mechanics and astronomy at the University of Padua from 1592 to 1610.

- Galileo built his first telescope in 1609, which featured three times magnification. Later, he developed models that could see up to 30 times magnification.

- Galileo was a well-known and accomplished musician.

- He published his first astronomical observations in 1610. The collection was called "Starry Messenger."

- Galileo also was one of the first people to observe sunspots, which helped develop the predictions that would help identify annual patterns.

- Using his telescopes, he was able to identify that the Moon had mountains and craters, dispelling the belief that it was a perfect sphere.

- Later in his life, Galileo became blind.

Chapter - 7

GEORGE EASTMAN
(1854–1932)

George Eastman was an *American inventor, entre-preneur* and a *philanthropist*. He is remembered for his invention of **film roll**. He was the founder of *Eastman Kodak Company*.

George Eastman

Quick Learn

A philanthropist is a person who spends money on humanity and social work.

Biography

George Eastman was born on July 12, 1854 in Waterville, New York. At the age of eight years, he started attending a private school in Rochester. After his father's death in 1862, Eastman's family condition became poor and he left his studies to earn money.

Eastman's Film Roll

Discoveries and Inventions

Eastman patented his first film roll in the year

1884. This was the first film roll to be proven practical as it was a dry, transparent, and flexible, photographic film. With the advent of film roll, there came a pioneering change in the field of photography.

In 1888, Eastman invented the Kodak camera. It was the first camera designed especially for the film roll.

Eastman's Kodak Camera

His aim was to simplify photography so that even masses could do photography.

Did You Know?

"You press the button, we do the rest" was the advertising slogan for Eastman's Kodak Camera.

George Eastman founded the Eastman Kodak Company in Rochester, New York in the year 1892. This company produced good quality photography equipments as well as the film roll invented by Eastman. It was the first of its kind photography company. The Kodak camera came with the pre-loaded film roll with 100 exposures. A person could use the camera and after finishing his role, he could hand it back to the company. The company then removed the film roll, developed the photographs and inserted a new film roll before handing back the camera. Eastman's commercial, transparent film roll formed the basis of Thomas Edison's motion picture camera.

Apart from photographic revolution, Eastman is also fondly remembered for his charitable work. He donated money for the building of educational and health institutes. He donated to the Massachusetts Institute of Technology and also contributed for the establishment of the Eastman School of Music in 1918 and a school of medicine and dentistry in 1921 at the University of Rochester.

George Eastman died of gunshot on March 14, 1932.

Scientists, Inventions and Discoveries

Quick Facts

- George Eastman was the first person to make the handheld Kodak camera.

- George Eastman's life in photography spans the half-century from 1880 to 1930, when science, technology and culture converged to create "new products" of all sorts.

- Eastman had built a "Method and Apparatus for Coating Plates" which made dry film a reality.

- In his final two years, Eastman was in intense pain caused by a degenerative disorder affecting his spine.

Chapter - 8

SIR ISAAC NEWTON
(1642–1727)

Sir Isaac Newton was an English astronomer, physicist, philosopher and mathematician. He is regarded as the greatest scientist ever. He is famous for his laws of motion and the concept of gravitation.

Sir Isaac Newton

Biography

Sir Isaac Newton was born on December 25, 1642 in Lincolnshire, England. Newton was named after his father – Isaac Newton, who died three months before his birth. He was a premature child and was raised by his maternal grandmother. Newton went to The King's School, Grantham when he turned 12. In 1661, he enrolled with the Trinity College, Cambridge. He obtained his degree in 1665. Later, he joined the same college as a Mathematics professor.

Newton was knighted by Queen Anne in London in 1705 for his contribution in the field of science.

Why was 'Sir' added before a name?

Being knighted means to have the title, 'Sir' before one's name. Therefore, some scientists had 'Sir' before their names.

Discoveries and Inventions

Newton's law of gravity – Newton stated that every object in the universe experiences a pull towards every other object. This amount of pull or force depends upon the masses of the objects and the distance between them.

Did You Know?

Newton was sitting under an apple tree when an apple fell down from the tree and hit him on the head. This made him wonder why the apple fell down instead of falling in any other direction. And this is how the law of gravity came into light.

Newton gave three laws of motion. They are:

Gravitational Force

- ☀ **First Law:** It states that a stationary object will remain in rest until an external force puts it in motion and an object in motion will continue to be in uniform motion (same speed and same direction) until an external force acts upon it to change the speed or the direction. This is also called as the Inertia of Rest or the Inertia of Motion.

- ☀ **Second Law:** It states that more the mass of the object, the more is the force required to move that object.

● **Third Law:** It states that every action has an equal and opposite reaction.

Newton's laws of motion are the basis of some of the most advanced techniques and technologies in use today. These were first published in **1687**, titled **Principia**. Apart from these, he also proposed the Newton's theory of colour. He also did some important work in optics.

Sir Isaac Newton died on March 31, 1727 during his sleep.

Quick Facts

- Newton chose to live a life of celibacy, and he never married.

- Newton was always interested in how things worked. As a young boy at Woolsthorpe, Newton constructed sundials accurate within fifteen minutes.

- Newton also invented the Calculus and explained the visible spectrum of light.

Chapter - 9

LOUIS PASTEUR
(1822–1895)

Louis Pasteur was a French chemist and microbiologist. He is known for his significant contribution towards microbiology and is often regarded as the father of modern microbiology because of his many contributions to science. He created the first vaccines for rabies and anthrax.

Louis Pasteur

Biography

Louis Pasteur was born in a tanner family on December 27, 1822 in Dole, France. He was a degree holder in mathematical sciences and joined the École Normale Supérieure College for higher studies. In 1848, he joined Dijon Lycée as a physics professor and later the University of Strasbourg as a professor of chemistry.

Pasteur had five children but only two of them survived. The other three died of typhoid. This personal grief led Pasteur to find about the cures to such life-threatening diseases.

Discoveries and Inventions

Louis Pasteur was the first to observe that day-to-day processes, like souring of beer, wine and milk, happen because of micro-organisms present in our atmosphere. After a series of experiments and observations, he found out that if we heat these affected liquids, then we can successfully remove

Sour Milk

these micro organisms (germs). This process of heating liquids to remove harmful micro organisms is known as **pasteurisation**.

Louis Pasteur also mentioned that not only these germs affect things like wine, beer, milk but also affect human beings and cause certain diseases. He studied the chickens suffering from chicken cholera and observed that if a cure for this disease can be found, then cures for other diseases caused by micro organisms can also be found.

Did You Know?

Doctors and surgeons sanitize their hands and equipments before and after every surgery. This practice was encouraged by Louis Pasteur because of his study of germs.

He also found out about the immunisation in a living being. He explained that when a living being is attacked by the same germ second time, his/ her body develops some amount of resistance towards the effects of that germ. This way, the germ is not able to cause serious infection to the living being. This resistance is known as the immune power of that living being.

Based on this immune power, Pasteur created vaccines for anthrax and rabies.

Quick Facts

- In the honour of his work and influential contributions, Louis Pasteur was made a Grand Croix of the Legion of Honour, a prestigious French order.

- He is well known for inventing a process to stop food and liquid, such as milk from making people sick. This method is called Pasteurisation. It helps to reduce the number of micro-organisms that could cause diseases while not affecting quality and taste in a way which sterilization would.

- Micro-organisms are very tiny organisms that harm living beings by attacking any weak spot in their bodies. The harmful ones are called germs like different types of bacteria and viruses.

- Many of Pasteur's experiments supported the germ theory of disease, and they helped show that micro-organisms are the true cause of many diseases. In earlier times, people believed that diseases were spontaneously generated. However, over time this theory was superseded — thanks to the work of Pasteur and many others.

Chapter - 10

MICHAEL FARADAY
(1791–1867)

Michael Faraday was an English physicist famous for his contribution in the field of physics and chemistry. The SI unit of capacitance is named 'Farad' to honour his contribution in the field of electromagnetism.

Michael Faraday

Biography

Michael Faraday was born on September 22, 1791 in Hampshire, England into a poor family. He was the third of four children and had very little basic education. When he was 14 years old, he became an apprentice with a local bookseller. It was here that he started reading books and found an inclination towards science. He started reading books on physics and chemistry and tried to apply the principles and suggestions of the books. Due to his correspondence with eminent scholars in these fields, he was appointed as a Chemical Assistant at the Royal Institution in 1813. This way he began the journey of his scientific exploration.

Did You Know?

Every Christmas, as a chemistry professor, Faraday used to give science lectures to a group of children from all age groups at the Royal Institution in London, England. These lectures grew very popular among the audiences and as a tradition, they are continued even today.

Discoveries and Inventions

Faraday's Generator

Faraday is famous for his work on **electromagnets**. He was the one to state the **law of induction**. He observed that electricity could be generated by moving a piece of magnet continuously inside a metal wire coil. Based on this, he built the first basic electric motor, transformer and generator. His observations of electromagnetic induction led to the principles of converting mechanical energy into electrical energy.

Faraday is famous for laying the basis of the electric generator. Through this generator, one can convert mechanical energy to electrical energy.

He is also credited for discovering the laws of electrolysis. These laws and principles find applications in many industrial purposes like separating certain metals from their ores to obtain pure metals. Similarly, batteries used in gadgets like remote controls are based on electrolysis.

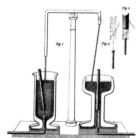

Electromagnetic Rotation

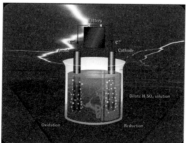

Faraday's Laws of Electrolysis

Induction Experiment

Quick Facts

- Faraday was the son of a poor blacksmith, born in the village of Newington in Surrey, England.

- Until 1830, Faraday was mainly a chemist. In 1825, he discovered an important chemical, Benzene.

- Using his discovery of electric induction, Faraday made the first dynamo to generate electricity and so opened the way to the modern age of electricity.

Chapter - 11

MARIE CURIE
(1867–1934)

Marie Curie was a Polish physicist and chemist, known worldwide for her findings on radioactive substances. Often referred to as Madam Curie and Dr. Curie, she is the first person to win two Nobel Prizes – one in physics and the other in chemistry.

Marie Curie

Biography

Marie Curie was born as Maria Salomea Skłodowska on November 7, 1867 in Warsaw, Kingdom of Poland to teacher parents. Curie worked as a governess for two years, assisting her sister to complete her college education. In the year 1890, she joined a laboratory at the Museum of Industry and Agriculture to begin her practical scientific training. In 1891, Marie left for France to join her sister and enrolled with the Sorbonne (University of Paris) to study Physics, Chemistry and Mathematics.

Discoveries and Inventions

Madam Curie observed that uranium emitted rays similar to X-rays and some harmful properties of these rays were indeed helpful to eradicate tumour. She along with her husband, Pierre Curie, discovered two new radioactive elements 'polonium' and 'radium'. For this, they both were given the Nobel Prize in Physics, in the year 1901. These names were coined by both of them together – Polonium on Poland, the birth land of Marie and Radium was named so because of his intense radioactivity. Even after her

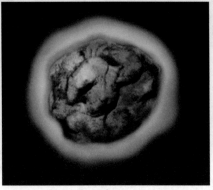

Radium

husband's death, she continued working on radioactive substances. In 1911, Marie Curie was honoured with a second Nobel Prize in Chemistry for successfully isolating pure radium and determining radium's atomic weight.

Did You Know?

Madam Curie was unaware of the dangers of radioactivity. She used to carry test tubes of radioactive substances in her coat pockets and stored them in her desk drawers. Her papers and books, kept in her laboratory – Musée Curie - are highly radioactive and are kept in protective boxes for the visitors to see.

Madam Curie died on July 4, 1934 in Poland due to constant exposure to radioactive substances.

Quick Facts

- A radioactive substance is that which emits rays due to chemical reactions within its atoms. These substances are dangerous to handle without proper protection as they emit huge amount of rays, harmful for the body.

- Marie Curie was the first woman to win two Nobel Prizes in Science—both in Physics and Chemistry.

- Marie Curie fainted from hunger because she was so engrossed in her studies that she forgot to eat or drink properly for days together.

- She invented the term, radioactivity.

- She was proud of being Polish and named the first element she discovered after her homeland – Polonium.

Chapter - 12

THOMAS ALVA EDISON
(1847–1931)

Thomas Alva Edison or Thomas Edison is the man who invented electric bulbs used to light our homes. He was an American inventor and businessman.

Biography

Thomas Edison was born on February 11, 1847 in Milan, Ohio as the seventh and last child to his parents, Samuel Ogden Edison and Nancy Matthews Elliott. He grew up in Port Huron, Michigan. He went to school for only three months and dropped out because he couldn't concentrate on his studies. He started doing little jobs like selling newspapers, candies and vegetables to supplement his chemical

Thomas Alva Edison

experiments. A few years later, he started a newspaper Grand Trunk Herald and with this, he started his career as a businessman. Edison had developed a hearing problem early in his life. However, this didn't deter him from continuing his research work.

Edison's Gifts

General Electric (GE), a successful multinational company was founded by Thomas Edison in 1890. You must have seen GE bulbs in the market. These are Edison's gifts to humanity.

Discoveries and Inventions

Edison's Electric Lamp

Edison began his career as an inventor in the year, **1877** with a **phonograph**. It is the basic version of the same device which we know as a **gramophone** and is used to play and record sounds.

In **1879**, Edison was able to produce a **light bulb**, using lower current electricity, a small carbonised filament and an improved vacuum inside the glass bulb. This bulb was a long-lasting and reliable source of electric light. After working on this experiment for one and a half years or more, Edison came up with an incandescent light bulb which was safe, economical and practical to use.

Edison's Light Bulb

Edison's Phonograph

Edison received his first patent on an electric vote recorder, a device intended for use by elected bodies to speed the voting process.

Did You Know?

Thomas Edison holds a record of having 1093 patents against his name in America alone. He also has many patents in United Kingdom, France and Germany.

Thomas Edison died on October 18, 1931 due to diabetic complications at his house in New Jersey, USA.

Quick Facts

- Edison was deaf and he liked it that way!

- He set up the world's first electric light power station in Lower Manhattan.

- Thomas Edison was famous for the following words, 'Genius is one percent inspiration, 99 percent perspiration'.

- He also invented the carbon microphone between the period, 1877-1878. This was used in all the telephones.

- His mother imparted him the basic education, teaching him reading, writing, and arithmetic. She also read to him from well-known English writers, such as Edward Gibbon, William Shakespeare, and Charles Dickens.

- Among his most important inventions were the electric light, the phonograph, and the motion-picture camera.

- The period from 1879 to 1900 is called the Age of Edison as this was the time span when he produced and perfected most of his devices.

S. CHANDRASEKHAR
(1910–1995)

S. Chandrasekhar or Subrahmanyan Chandrasekhar was an eminent Indian-American astrophysicist. He was honoured with a **Nobel Prize for Physics** in **1983**. He is world famous for giving the 'Chandrasekhar Limit'.

S. Chandrasekhar

Biography

S. Chandrasekhar was born on October 19, 1910 in Lahore, Punjab. He was the nephew of Nobel laureate physicist Sir C. V. Raman. Initially tutored at home, Chandrasekhar attended the Hindu High School, Madras (Chennai) from 1922-25. From 1925-1930, he studied at the Presidency College, Chennai. In 1930, the Government of India awarded a scholarship to him for pursuing graduation in the University of Cambridge. He joined the Trinity College and in 1933, Chandrasekhar got his Ph.D. degree from Cambridge. He was elected to a prize fellowship at the university for four years (1933-1937).

Discoveries and Inventions

From 1929 to 1939, Chandrasekhar studied the stellar structure. From 1943 to 1950, he studied the theory of radiative transfer and the quantum theory of negative ion of hydrogen.

A White Dwarf Star

From 1950 to 1961, Chandrasekhar worked upon hydrodynamics and hydro genetic stability. He studied the mathematic theory of black holes from 1971 to 1983 and after that concentrated on the theory of colliding gravitational waves.

He is famous for his Chandrasekhar limit. It is defined as the maximum mass of a stable white dwarf star.

S. Chandrasekhar was awarded the Nobel Prize for Physics in 1983 for his studies on the physical processes important to the structure and evolution of stars. He was also honoured with the Padma Vibhushan in 1968.

S. Chandrasekhar died on August 21, 1995 in Chicago, USA.

Quick Facts

- A white dwarf star is a star which is about to extinguish in a few years. It is a final evolutionary stage of a star – beyond which it will not evolve.

- Chandrasekhar, known simply as "Chandra" in the scientific world, was one of ten children of Chandrasekhara Subrahmanyan Ayyar and Sitalakshmi Balakrishnan. Ayyar was an officer in the British government services. Sitalakshmi, a woman of great talent and self-taught intellectual attainments, played a pivotal role in her son's career.

- Chandrasekhar's uncle, Sir Chandrasekhara Venkata Raman was the recipient of a Nobel Prize for the celebrated discovery concerning the molecular scattering of light known as the "Raman Effect."

- He, too was awarded the Nobel Prize in Physics in 1983 for his studies on the physical processes important to the structure and evolution of stars. Chandrasekhar accepted this honour but was upset that the citation mentioned only his earliest work, seeing it as a denigration of a lifetime's achievement. He shared it with William A. Fowler.

- Chandrasekhar was the managing editor of the Astrophysical Journal from 1952 to 1971. He converted essentially a private journal of the University of Chicago into a national journal of the American Astronomical Society.

Chapter - 14

DR. VIKRAM SARABHAI
(1919–1971)

Hailed as the Father of the Indian Space Program, Dr. Vikram Sarabhai was an eminent Indian physicist.

Biography

Born on August 12, 1919 in Ahmedabad, Gujarat as Vikram Ambalal Sarabhai, he was the son of a wealthy family. His father, Ambalal Sarabhai was a rich industrialist and owned many mills.

Dr. Vikram Sarabhai

Vikram Sarabhai completed his secondary education from the Gujarat College, Ahmedabad after he passed his intermediate Science Examination. He next joined St. John's College, University of Cambridge, England. In 1940, he received the Tripos from the Cambridge University. He came back to India and joined the Indian Institute of Science, with the escalation of the World War II.

Discoveries and Inventions

At the Indian Institute of Science, Bangalore, presently called Bengaluru, Sarabhai started his research work in Cosmic Rays. He did his research under the guidance of his uncle, the eminent physicist, Sir C. V. Raman.

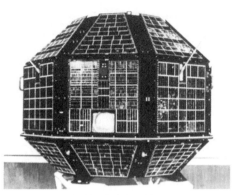

The Satellite, Aryabhata

He was offered a Doctor of Research Degree at the University of Cambridge for his thesis titled Cosmic Ray Investigation in Tropical Latitudes, in 1947. He returned back to Cambridge in 1945 after the end of the war. In his thesis, he observed that there were immense opportunities opening up in solar as well as interplanetary physics.

Dr. Sarabhai returned to India after the Indian Independence. He played a significant role in establishing the Physical Research Laboratory in Ahmedabad in November, 1947. He also established many other educational institutions like the Indian Institute of Management (IIM), Centre for Environmental Planning and Technology (CEPT), Blind Men Association.

Dr. Sarabhai set up the First Rocket Launching Setup (TERLS) in Thumba, Kerala with the help of Dr. Homi Jehangir Bhabha. The Satellite Instructional Television Experiment (SITE) was launched during 1975-76 as a result of his conversation with NASA in 1966. Aryabhatta, the first Indian satellite was put in orbit in 1975 as a result of Dr. Sarabhai`s project. He was very interested in science education and founded a Community Science Centre at Ahmedabad in 1966.

Vikram Sarabhai died on December 30, 1971 at Kovalam in Kerala.

Quick Facts

- Padma awards are the highest civilian awards of India.

- Vikram Sarabhai did research on the time variations of cosmic rays.

- He also visualised a new field of research opening up in Solar and was awarded `Dr. Shanti Swarup Bhatnagar Prize` in the year, 1962. He was conferred with the Padma Shri Award in 1966 and was awarded Padma Vibhushan in 1972.

- He was also appointed Chairman of the Atomic Energy Commission in May 1966 after the death of Dr. Homi Jehangir Bhabha.

- In the year, 1942, Vikram Sarabhai married Mrinalini Sarabhai, who was a famous classical dancer.

Chapter - 15

SIR JAGDISH CHANDRA BOSE
(1858–1937)

Sir or Acharya Jagadish Chandra Bose was an Indian physicist, biologist, botanist and archaeologist. He is well reputed for his contribution towards plant science and his research work in the field of radio and microwave optics. He is also well known for the invention of Crescograph. Dr. J. C. Bose was honoured with the title of 'Sir' after he was knighted in 1916 by the British government.

Sir Jagdish Chandra Bose

Biography

Dr. J. C. Bose was born on November 13, 1858 in Bikrampur, Bengal (now Bangladesh). He completed his primary education in a local school and then joined St. Xavier's School, Kolkata. Later on he got admission in St. Xavier's College, Kolkata. He then moved to England and got admission in Christ College, University of Cambridge to study natural sciences. In 1885, Bose returned to India and joined the Presidency College as the officiating professor of Physics.

Discoveries and Inventions

Bose's most celebrated research was the discovery of the fact that plants respond to various stimuli. He demonstrated the response to stimulation between living and non-living.

His contribution in plant science is phenomenal. Through various experiments, he proved that plants grow faster with pleasant music and

Crescograph

gets stagnated amidst harsh sounds. He invented the **crescograph**, a device made to measure the growth in plants.

In the year 1894, Bose demonstrated short-wave communication by performing an experiment is which he rang a bell at a distance using milimetre wave (microwaves in millimetre length). He also made these microwaves ignite gunpowder.

His work on wireless communication found him an American patent and made him the first Indian to receive a patent from America. Bose is also regarded as the inventor of wireless telegraphy.

In 1895, Bose's first scientific paper titled 'On polarisation of electric rays by double refracting crystals' was communicated to the Asiatic Society of Bengal.

Sir J. C. Bose was also a writer. He is regarded as the first Bengali Science fiction writer. He wrote a science fiction piece of work named, 'Niruddesher Kahani' in Bengali in 1896.

Bose died on November 23, 1937.

Quick Facts

- A stimulus or stimuli (plural) is an external substance or force which affects an activity.

- The year, 2008 was marked as the 150th birth anniversary of Sir Jagadish Chandra Bose who, at a relatively young age, established himself among the ranks of European scientists during the heyday of colonial rule in India.

- Bose's experiments were carried out at the Presidency College in Calcutta (Kolkata), although for demonstrations he developed a compact portable version of the equipment, including transmitter, receiver and various microwave components called the Bose's Apparatus. Some of his original equipment still exists, now at the Bose Institute in Kolkata.

Chapter - 16

SIR C. V. RAMAN
(1888–1970)

Sir C. V. Raman or Chandrasekhara Venkata Raman was an eminent **Indian physicist**. He was a **Nobel laureate** who received this coveted honour for his work titled the **'Raman effect'**.

Biography

Sir Chandrasekhara Venkata Raman was born in Thiruvanaikaval near Tiruchirappalli of Madras Presidency on November 7, 1888. Madras is presently known as Chennai. Raman moved to Andhra Pradesh to study in St. Aloysius Anglo-Indian High School at a very early age. At the age of 13, in 1902, Raman entered the Presidency College, Madras. He passed his Bachelor's in Physics with a gold medal in the year, 1904 and in 1907, Raman passed his Master's with distinction.

Sir C.V. Raman

In 1917, Sir C. V. Raman took the Professorship in Physics at the University of Calcutta. Simultaneously, he continued his studies at the Indian Association for the Cultivation of Science. In 1934, he became the Director of the Indian **Institute of Science, Bangalore**, presently known as **Bengaluru**. Dr. C. V. Raman established a company called the Travancore Chemical and Manufacturing Company Ltd. in 1943 along with Dr. Krishnamurthy. He was conferred the British knighthood in the year 1929 and was thereafter known as Sir C. V. Raman.

Discoveries and Inventions

Sir C. V. Raman discovered the 'Raman effect' on February 28, 1928 while going through his experiment on the scattering of light.

Raman's Spectroscopy is a spectroscopic method used in Physics and Chemistry to study vibration, rotational and other low-frequency modes in a system.

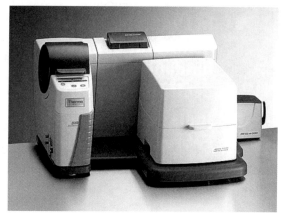

Raman's Spectrometer

He also worked on the traverse vibration of bow strings. He was the first one to investigate the harmonic sound of Indian instruments like tabla and mridanga.

Dr. C. V. Raman got worldwide reputation for his work in scattering of light and optics. In 1930, Sir C. V. Raman won the Nobel Prize for Physics for his work on scattering of light – the Raman Effect. He was also honoured with **Bharat Ratna** in **1954** and with the **Lenin Peace Prize** in the year **1957**.

Sir C. V. Raman died on November 21, 1970, aged 82.

Quick Facts

🗣 C.V. Raman and another Indian scientist Suri Bhagavantam discovered the quantum photon spin in 1932, which confirmed the quantum nature of light.

🗣 Raman also worked on the acoustics of musical instruments.

🗣 In 1948, Raman, through studying the spectroscopic behaviour of crystals, approached in a new manner fundamental problems of crystal dynamics. He also dealt with the structure and properties of diamond.

🗣 India celebrates the National Science Day on February 28 of every year to commemorate the

INVENTIONS AND DISCOVERIES

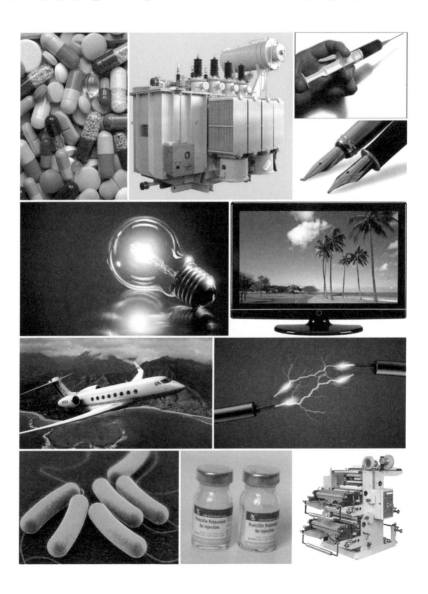

Chapter - 1

BACTERIA

Bacteria are one of the *micro-organisms* which populate the planet, earth. Mostly a few micrometres in size, bacteria are found in many different shapes like spheres, rods, spirals. Bacteria are about *1000 nanometres in size*. (A nanometre is one-millionth of a millimetre).

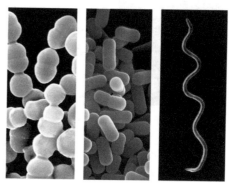
Bacteria of Different Shapes

They are present in most of the habitats on the earth, in every climate and region. They are found in soil, water, air and even inside the earth's crust. They are also found in organic matter and on the bodies of other living organisms.

Did You Know?

There are around 40 million bacteria in a gram of soil and around one million in a millimetre of freshwater.

Antonie Van Leeuwenhoek

Bacteria were first found by Antonie Van Leeuwenhoek in the year, 1667 with the help of a single lens microscope. He was the first microbiologist in the history of science and he made this discovery using the microscope of his own design. He named the micro-organisms 'animalcules'. Later, he published his discovery in the Letters to the Royal Society.

Antonie Van Leeuwenhoek

Did You Know?

The name, **bacterium** was coined by **Christian Gottfried Ehrenberg** in **1828**.

Single-celled bacteria were the first form of life to appear on planet Earth around four million years back. They are an important part of the earth's evolution. They help in many natural processes like secreting enzymes for natural decay, recycling nutrients, dissolving complex compounds.

Ehrenberg

There are millions of bacteria in a human body. Some are made ineffectual by the immune system of the body, some are good for human health, while some are infection-causing too. Certain bacteria found in things like curd, yeast are good for the human digestive system. But some bacteria cause life threatening diseases like cholera, anthrax, diarrhoea.

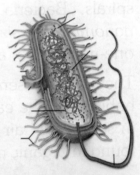
A Bacterial Cell

Quick Facts

- The study of bacteria is known as **Bacteriology**. It is a branch of **Microbiology**.

- **Different bacteria can live at a huge range of temperatures, from ice or snow to hot springs, and can even live in radioactive waste.**

- Most bacteria are useful – gut bacteria produce vitamins that help human beings and animals digest their food, and bacteria in the roots help legumes (plants in the pea and bean family) get nitrogen out of the soil, which helps them to grow.

- Bacteria are used in making cheese, yoghurt and sourdough bread.

- Bacteria produce oxygen – perhaps as much as half of the oxygen in the atmosphere.

- Bacteria (usually dead or weak ones) are used to make vaccines.

- Bacteria are used to clean water in sewage plants.

- Bacteria can cause food poisoning (sickness and diarrhoea) - this is why chicken needs to be cooked thoroughly, and why some food should be kept in the fridge.

- Bacterial infections can be cured with antibiotics – drugs that kill bacteria.

Chapter - 2

VITAMINS

A vitamin is an organic compound. It is an important nutrient required in an organism for living healthily. The word, vitamin is derived from 'vitamine' by Polish scientist Casimir Funk. Vitamine was made up of words – vital and amine.

In other words, a vitamin is an organic compound which cannot be produced in the human body and is derived from other sources like vegetables, fruits, sunlight, milk. Vitamins are needed in a very small amount for the human body. Lack of necessary vitamins cause certain defects and weaknesses in human beings.

Vitamin K1

There are a number of different types of vitamins which have different functions to promote health. They are vitamin **A, B1, B2, B3, B5, B6, B7, B9, B12, C, D, E** and **K**. Some vitamins act to control the metabolism rate, some regulate the growth of the body, and some help in maintaining the immune system.

Until 1930, the only source of vitamins was food intake. Since then, vitamins have been extracted from their natural sources and sold as food supplement tablets at very cheap rates.

Frederick Gowland Hopkins

Frederick Gowland Hopkins or Sir F. G. Hopkins is known as the 'Father of British Biochemistry'. He was the one who firmly established the existence of vitamins in certain food items. He observed that there was something more than proteins, carbohydrates, minerals and fats in a balanced diet of food which keeps the body healthy. He and other scientist concluded, there were altogether different nutrients required for maintenance of a living organism.

Frederick Gowland Hopkins

F.G. Hopkins was knighted in the year, 1925 as Sir F. G. Hopkins and in 1929, he shared the Nobel Prize in Physiology and Medicine with Christiaan Ejikman for their discovery of growth stimulating vitamins.

Did You Know?

Intake of Vitamin C helps in strengthening immunity and helps in reducing the effects of cough and common cold. Citrus fruits are the best natural sources of Vitamin C.

It is a fact that consumption of vitamins that exceeds from what is required can cause overdose and side effects and it is also true that deficiency of vitamins from what is required causes diseases and medical ailments. So below is a list of top ten essential vitamins with their sources and deficiencies, overdose and side effects. Knowledge of all these will help you determine which food sources provide which types of vitamins and deficiency, and overdose of which vitamins cause what type of medical diseases. This simple but complete guide of top ten vitamins will help you in building a healthy and balanced diet, which will be full of nutrition.

Food Sources of Vitamin A

Meat, eggs, cheese, milk, cream, kidney, liver and cod liver oil, all these, except for skimmed milk are high in saturated fat and cholesterol and are sources of Vitamin A. Carrots are a rich source of Vitamin A.

Milk

Egg

Meat

Deficiencies, Overdose, And Side Effects of Vitamin A

Deficiency of Vitamin A can cause vision problems and increases susceptibility to infectious diseases. Overdose of Vitamin A can cause birth defects. Acute vitamin A poisoning can occur when an adult takes several hundred thousand units of vitamin A supplements per day.

Food Sources of Vitamin B12

Beef, poultry, eggs, seafood and milk and its derivatives contain Vitamin B12.

Vitamin B12 deficiency occurs when the body is unable to absorb it from the intestinal tract, which may be caused due to pernicious anaemia (decreased red blood cells). Lower levels of Vitamin B12 can cause anaemia, numbness or tingling in the arms and legs along with weakness and loss of balance.

Poultry (Hen)

Milk

Eggs

Food Sources of Vitamin B6

Nuts, beans, legumes, meat, eggs, fish, enriched breads, cereals and whole grains are some sources of Vitamin B6.

Deficiencies, Side Effects and Overdose of Vitamin B6

Vitamin B6 overdose can cause neurological disorders, weakness, and numbness. Deficiency of Vitamin B6 can cause ulcers of the mouth and tongue, irritability, confusion, anxiety and depression.

Deficiencies, Side Effects and Overdose of Vitamin B6

Deficiency of Vitamin B6 causes pellagra and the symptoms of pellagra include inflammation of the skin, mental deterioration and digestive problems. Overdose of Vitamin B6 can cause peptic ulcer disease, liver damage and skin rash. Even normal doses can be associated with the reddening of the skin.

Food Sources of Vitamin B1

Cereals, breads, pasta, lean meats (especially pork), fish, whole grains (especially wheat germ) dry beans, soybean, and peas contain vitamin B1.

Breads and Buns

Cereals (Whole Grains)

Fish

Vitamin B1 Deficiency

Deficiency of Vitamin B1 can cause fatigue, weakness, nerve damage, and psychosis. Excessive consumption of alcohol impairs absorption of this vitamin, which can lead to the development of a disease called beriberi (may affect cardiovascular or nervous system).

Food Sources of Vitamin B3

Poultry, dairy, fish, nuts, lean meat, and eggs contain vitamin B3. Cereals also supply some of this vitamin.

Egg   *Red Meat*   *Fish*   *Dairy Products*   *Hen (Chicken)*   *Nuts*

Food Sources of Biotin

Fish, eggs, dairy products including milk, curd, butter, legumes, whole grains, broccoli yeast, some vegetables in the cabbage family, sweet potatoes, and lean meat contain biotin.

Butter   Curd   Legumes and Nuts   Milk   Food Grains

Overdose of Biotin

Overdose of Biotin or Pantothenic acid produces symptoms of possible diarrhoea.

Food Sources of Vitamin C

Citrus fruits and juices, tomatoes, strawberries, broccoli, sweet potatoes, papaya, cantaloupe, cauliflower, Brussels sprouts, cabbage, raspberries, blueberries, and pineapple contain vitamin C. Also one citrus orange contains 45 mg of Vitamin C.

Citrus Fruits   Tomatoes   Strawberries   Broccoli   Sweet Potatoes

Vitamin C Overdose and Side Effects

Amounts exceeding 2,000 mg/day of vitamin C supplements can lead to stomach upset and diarrhoea. A small amount can cause inflammation and bleeding of the gums, rough and dry skin, decreased rate of wound healing and so on.

Food Sources of Vitamin D

Fish, dairy products, fortified cereals, oysters and margarine are some Vitamin D rich foods.

Fish   *Dairy Products*   *Fortified Cereals*   *Oysters*

Deficiencies, Overdose and Side Effects of Vitamin D

Deficiency of Vitamin D causes osteoporosis in old people and rickets in children. Overdose of Vitamin D causes undesirable effect that starts removing calcium from the bones and place them into other vital organs like heart and lungs, thereby reducing their overall capacity and function.

Food Sources of Vitamin E

Corn, wheat germ, seeds, nuts, spinach, olives, vegetable oils, asparagus, sunflower, corn, soybean, and cottonseed contain high levels of Vitamin E.

Corn   *Wheat Germ*   *Seeds & Nuts*   *Spinach*   *Olives*   *Vegetable Oils*

Deficiencies, Side Effects and Overdose of Vitamin E

Overdose of Vitamin E at 400 International Units per day or more than that may increase the risk of death, but consuming multivitamins, which contain Vitamin E, is not harmful because of lose dose and quantity of vitamin E in the multivitamin supplements.

Food Sources of Vitamin K

Cauliflower   *Cabbage*   *Corn*   *Spinach*   *Soybeans*   *Vegetables*

Cauliflower, cabbage, corn, spinach, soybeans and other green vegetables contain Vitamin K. Vitamin K is absorbed by the bacteria that lines the gastrointestinal tract.

Vitamin K Deficiency

Deficiency of Vitamin K is very rare but it occurs when our body is unable to absorb vitamin K from the intestinal tract, which increases the chances of bleeding and bruising and uncontrolled bleeding because of the stoppage of normal clotting system which is essential for regularisation of the blood system.

Least but not last, it should be noted that only overdose of vitamins can cause side effects, but then also before taking these vitamins and to know the recommended dosages, you should consult with your family physician, dietician, or doctor of naturopathy.

Quick Facts

- Metabolism is the process of digesting the consumed food and deriving the required nutrients from it.
- A vitamin is an organic compound required as a nutrient in tiny amounts by an organism.
- Vitamin A was given the first letter of the alphabet, as it was the first to be discovered.

- Vitamins are classified as either water-soluble or fat-soluble. In humans, there are 13 vitamins: 4 fat-soluble (A, D, E and K) and 9 water-soluble (8 B vitamins and vitamin C).

- Vitamin C helps to slow down or prevent cell damage. Vitamin C is an antioxidant but is also vital for the production of collagen and enhances iron absorption.

- Vitamin E is a powerful antioxidant, neutralizing cell-damaging free radical in the body.

- Vitamin E also protects the skin from harmful effects of ultraviolet light.

- It has been proven that cancer is a deficiency disease caused by the lack of Vitamin B17 (Laetrile).

Chapter - 3

RABIES VACCINE

Rabies vaccine is a vaccination used to prevent and control rabies disease in humans and animals.

Rabies – The Disease

Rabies is an infectious disease caused by *rabies virus*. The rabies virus is a RNA virus which affects the *brain and the spinal cord*, in short the central nervous system, of humans as well as of animals. The virus travels from nerve cells to the brain of the mammal. On reaching the brain, it multiplies in

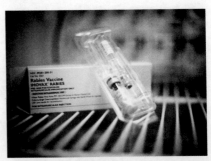
Rabies Vaccine

number and causes destruction of brain cells which causes death. The infection might become deadly if not treated well before the symptoms appear.

Structure of the Rabies Virus

The rabies viruses generally attack animals like *dogs, bats, skunks, foxes,* etc. It is through these animals that the disease gets spread

Rabies Virus

in *human beings*. As it is a communicable disease, the rabies virus spread through animal saliva or brain tissues. Mostly, it gets transmitted to human beings through dog bite. Rabies virus attacks the nervous system and the person starts having hallucinations, agitation, seizures, then finally coma and death. In animals, the symptoms usually are irritation, agitation and aggressive behaviour.

Louis Pasteur and Emile Roux

Louis Pasteur

Emile Roux

Prior to the discovery of the rabies vaccine, *every rabid-case would result in death.* In 1888, two French scientists, **Louis Pasteur** and **Emile Roux** developed the first rabies vaccine. Pasteur, unlike his many colleagues, did not follow the theory that 'diseases come from nowhere'. His main focus of work was to determine the causes behind various diseases.

Did You Know?

The rabies vaccine was first used on a *nine-year-old Joseph Meister on July 6, 1885*, who had been bitten by a rabid dog. *He was the first human being to be vaccinated by rabies vaccine.*

The Cure of Rabies

The rabies vaccine was made up of a sample of virus cultivated from infected and dead rabbit. The sample was weakened by allowing it to dry for a few days.

Pasteur observed that while transmitting rabies virus from one rabbit to another, the healthy rabbit did not become as sick as the first one. This meant that the rabies virus was weakening and injecting the healthy rabbit with the weak virus which gave immunity to the healthy rabbit.

Quick Facts

- Rabies occurs everywhere and kills at least 55,000 people per year.

- The rabies virus was not seen through a microscope until 1950s.

- Most human cases of rabies are due to transmission of the virus through dog bites. Other animals that can carry the rabies virus include cats, raccoons, skunks, bats and livestock.

- Early symptoms of rabies in humans are similar to flu, with fever and fatigue. The rabies virus then damages the central nervous and respiratory systems. The final stages may include paralysis or hyperactivity and then coma and death.

- If you are exposed to rabies, the wound or exposure should be cleaned and disinfected immediately. An anti-rabies vaccine must also be administered as soon as possible.

- Once the symptoms of rabies appear in humans, no treatment is possible, and the infected person almost always dies within a week.

PENICILLIN

Introduction

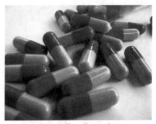

Penicillin Capsules

Penicillin is the world's one of the first antibiotic to be discovered. It is derived from a mold called penicillium. Discovery of penicillin pioneered a historic start in the field of antibiotics.

Before the discovery of penicillin, there were no cures for diseases like *pneumonia, gonorrhea, rheumatic fever*, etc. Antibiotics are compounds produced by *bacteria, fungi* and other *microscopic species* to counterattack other species.

Did You Know?

The development of penicillin has been regarded as an International Historical Chemical Landmark by *The American Chemical Society* and the *Royal Society of Chemistry*, on *November 19, 1999*.

Alexander Fleming

Alexander Fleming was a *Professor of Bacteriology* at *St. Mary's Hospital in London*. He discovered **Penicillin** in **1928**.

As a professor of bacteriology, Fleming studied different types of bacteria. Once, he was studying some bacteria which cause sore throats, boils, etc, he found that in one dish there is a blob of mold. Studying it further, he found out that the mold secreted some kind

Alexander Fleming

of substance which killed the bacteria surrounding it. Thus, he observed that mold had some kind of substance which reduces the growth of infection-causing bacteria.

Howard Florey

Later, penicillium research shifted to Oxford University. In 1940, Howard Florey, a scientist at Sir William Dunn School of Pathology, observed that penicillin can protect mice from a death-causing bacteria infection.

However, this research yet couldn't be used for mass welfare as it needed a large quantity of this mold culture. Florey, along with Norman Heatley, came to US with a small amount of penicillin, during the war days.

Production of Penicillin

A process of producing large quantity of penicillium mold was found out. Air was pumped into deep vats of corn steep liquour (a byproduct of milling process). To produce this vaccine other key ingredients were mixed, which resulted in faster growth of penicillin in a large amount.

However, it was a small amount of penicillin found in a moldy cantaloupe in a Peoria market, which was used for mass production of the antibiotic.

Quick Facts

- Antibiotics are natural substances released by bacteria and fungi to safeguard themselves.
- Bacteriology is the study of bacteria.

Some of the side effects of Penicillin are:

- Diarrhoea that is watery or bloody
- Fever, chills, body aches, flu symptoms
- Easy bruising or bleeding, unusual weakness
- Urinating less than usual or not at all
- Severe skin rashes, itching, or peeling
- Agitation, confusion, unusual thoughts or behaviour
- Seizure (black-outs or convulsions)

AEROPLANE

Introduction

Aeroplane or Airplane is the *fastest means of transportation* today.

Prior to airplanes, air travel was limited to gliders, hot air balloons, etc. But these were not successful commercially.

Since the advent of the air travel, many attempts have been made to manufacture an efficient and affordable means of air transportation. With the invention of a power-propelled aircraft, the commercial scope of air travel has been met efficiently.

An Aeroplane

The Wright Brothers

In the year, **1903**, Wright brothers, **Orville and Wilbur** demonstrated the first ever airplane with a propeller. It was the first aircraft carrying a man, propelled by a machine which flew by its own power at an even speed and descended down without any damage. In the commercial sense, it was the basic design of an aircraft which would change the course of high speed transportation in the modern world.

The Wright brothers started with building and testing gliders. In the year 1900, they tested their new biplane glider weighing 50 pounds. Next year, they flew the largest glider ever but this one also faced problems. They conducted some tests and based on them, Wright brothers thought of building powered aircraft.

Their first airplane was named 'Flyer' which had a 12 horse powered engine.

Wright Brothers

After this airplane invention of Wright brothers, inventors started improving on these models and soon the world saw the advent of jet planes.

Working of an Aeroplane

An airplane flies on the basis of four things – thrust, drag, weight and lift. A propeller helps the plane to move forward with a high speed. This is called thrust. But the air in the atmosphere opposes the speed of the plane. This is called the drag. Thus, in order to move forward, thrust must be greater than

A Jet Plane

drag. Now, to move upwards in the sky, the plane needs to have a lift which can overcome the barrier of the plane's weight. For this purpose, wings are used. Airplane wings are curved from top and linear from below. Thus, air moves faster on top of the wing and slower below. This lifts the plane up in the air. The wings help in changing the direction of the plane by rolling on either side. By lifting up the nose, the pitch of the plane can be raised.

Quick Facts

- The pitch of the plane means to climb up or descend down.

- The first United States coast to coast airplane flight occurred in 1911 and took 49 days.

- An airplane's 'blackbox' is a device which records conditions and events on an air vessel. A 'blackbox' is actually orange in color to make it more visible in the wreckage. The term blackbox might come from its charred appearance after an air crash.

- The plane Boeing 747–400 has six million different parts, half of which are fasteners, made in 33 different countries.

- The outer skin of an aeroplane is only 5 mm thick. During takeoff, when full of high pressure air, the take-off weight is increased by about a ton.

Chapter - 6

ELECTRICITY

Electricity has fast become one of the basic needs today, along with air, water, food and shelter. It is a form of energy which is used to run appliances, devices, gadgets, machines – from the most basic ones to the advanced machines.

What is Electricity?

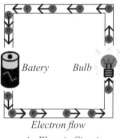

Batery   Bulb

Electron flow
An Electric Circuit

Electricity, in scientific terms, is the *flow of electrons*. When there is a continuous flow of electrons through a conductor like metal wire, then it is known as current. This current, in simple terms, is also known as electricity.

You can produce electric charge by rubbing one end of your ruler with wool. Rub it continuously for a few minutes. Then bring it near a piece of paper. You'll notice that the piece of paper would cling to the ruler. This shows that an electric charge has been developed at the end of the ruler, which is attracting the paper.

Benjamin Franklin

Benjamin Franklin was a *physicist* who is credited for discovering electricity. He is known for his famous kite experiment during which he observed that lightning is electricity. In June **1752**, he attached a metal key to the string of a kite and flew it in a rainy sky. He noticed that there were some sparks jumping towards his hand from the metal key. He deduced that after getting wet, the string became a good conductor and through this string, the electric charges in the atmosphere travelled to the metal key in the form of sparks.

Benjamin Franklin

Did You Know?

Lightning is the most dramatic effect of electricity.

This was a breakthrough. Franklin's experiment proposed the basic principles of electricity.

Later, these principles were applied in various fields of Physics like electromagnetism. Many great scientists based their research on these principles and invented the electric motor, electric bulb and many more electric devices.

Lightning

How is Electricity Produced?

The most basic device for producing electricity is a **generator**. Put a coil of copper wire between the poles of a magnet. Attach the copper wire ends to a shaft. On rotating the shaft, the copper wire coil would also rotate within the magnetic field. This produces electric current or electricity.

Electricity is the science, engineering, technology and physical phenomena associated with the presence and flow of electric charges. Electricity gives a wide variety of well-known electrical effects, such as lightning, static electricity, electromagnetic induction and the flow of electrical current in an electrical wire. In addition, electricity permits the creation and reception of electromagnetic radiation such as radio waves.

In electricity, charges produce electromagnetic fields which act on other charges. Electricity occurs due to several types of Physics:

- Electric charge: a property of some subatomic particles, which determines their electromagnetic interactions. Electrically charged matter is influenced by, and produces, electromagnetic fields.

- Electric current: a movement or flow of electrically charged particles, typically measured in amperes.

- Electric field: An especially simple type of electromagnetic field produced by an electric charge even when it is not moving (i.e., there is no electric current).

The electric field produces a force on other charges in its vicinity. Moving charges additionally produce a magnetic field.

- Electric potential: The capacity of an electric field to do work on an electric charge, typically measured in volts.

- Electromagnets: Electrical currents generate magnetic fields, and changing magnetic fields generate electrical currents.

In electrical engineering, electricity is used for:

- Electric power (which can refer imprecisely to a quantity of electrical potential energy or else more correctly to electrical energy per time) that is provided commercially, by the electrical power industry. In a loose but common use of the term, "electricity" may be used to mean "wired for electricity" which means a working connection to an electric power station. Such a connection grants the user of 'electricity' access to the electric field present in electrical wiring, and thus to electric power.

* Electronics deals with electrical circuits that involve active electrical components such as vacuum tubes, transistors, diodes and integrated circuits, and associated passive interconnection technologies.

Uses of Electricity

The present age is the age of electricity. Hence, we find various uses of electric power. The huge factories of heavy industries are easily run by electric current. Many railway trains, trams, buses and slips are moved by electric power. X-ray photos are also taken with the help of this power. Great surgical treatments are done in the darkest nights only with the help of this powerful electric light. Machines of the radio-set, television and telescope work with the help of this power. Electric power is used in lighting the public roads, waiting rooms, conferences and meetings. The cold-storage has been possible owing to this electric power. Medical wards and cinema houses are air-conditioned only with the help of electricity. Many people use this power to make their home life comfortable. Most of our articles of use are made in the factories run by the electric power. Hence, the uses of electricity are numerous.

Quick Facts

* Electric current is measured in amperes (amps).
* Electric potential energy is measured in volts.
* Two positive charges or two negative charges repel each other, whereas, two opposite charges on the other hand attract each other.
* When an electric charge builds up on the surface of an object, it creates static electricity.

- Electric eels can produce strong electric shocks of around 500 volts for both self-defence and hunting.
- Electricity travels at the speed of light – more than 186,000 miles per second!
- A spark of static electricity can measure up to 3,000 volts.
- Electric circuits can contain parts such as switches, transformers, resistors, etc.
- Electricity can be made from wind, water, the sun and even animal poop.
- A common way to produce electricity is by hydropower, a process that generates electricity by using water to spin turbines attached to generators.
- The world's biggest source of energy for producing electricity comes from coal. The burning of coal in furnaces heats the boiler water until it becomes steam which then spins turbines attached to the generators.

Chapter - 7

CINEMA

Introduction

Cinema is the most widely acclaimed means of entertainment in the world today. It is a combination of various equipments, techniques and art which constitutes cinema.

But the most important things needed to experience cinema are *camera, film reel* and a *projector*. **'Wheel of life'** or **'zoopraxiscope'** was the first machine to show animated pictures. It was patented in 1867 by **William Lincoln**. In a zoopraxiscope, moving photographs were watched through a slit.

A Zoopraxiscope

The Lumière Brothers

"The cinema is an invention without a future." – Louis Lumière. The Lumiere brothers – **Auguste** and **Louise** - are credited for inventing the first motion picture camera in the year, **1895**. But even prior to Lumiere brothers, many others had made similar inventions. Lumiere brothers

Auguste and Louise Lumiere

invented a *portable motion-picture camera*, film processing unit and a projector called the **Cinematographe**. Here, three functions were covered in one invention.

Lumiere's Cinematographe

Did You Know?

The first footage shot by Lumiere brothers was that of workers leaving the Lumiere factory.

Cinematographe or Cinematography brought a revolutionary

Edison's Vitascope

change in the world of cinema and made motion pictures popular. Though, prior to 1891, the Edison Company came up with a kinetoscope which allowed to watch cinema one person at a time, Edison's vitascope (1896) was the first commercially successful projector in USA.

Working of Cinema

The cinema constitutes of equipments, techniques and art. A camera shoots an activity on a *film roll*, also known as *a film negative*. This film negative is then edited. An editor removes away unnecessary scenes by cutting away that portion of the film role. Then the edited film roll is processed in a lab with required effects. The final film

footage is then mounted on a *projector*. A projector is a device which projects the film running on the film roll on a blank white screen with the help of light.

There are *two pulleys* on a projector. The film reel is mounted on the first projector and is run through the first to the second projector with the help of a motor. The film

A Film Projector

reel passes between a magnifying lens and a light bulb. The lens increases the size of the image on the blank white screen.

Cinematography is an art form unique to *motion pictures*. Although the exposing of images on light-sensitive elements dates back to the early 19th century, motion pictures demanded a new form of photography and new aesthetic techniques. In the early stage of motion pictures, the cinematographer was usually the director and the person physically handling the camera. As the art form and technology evolved, a separation between the director and the camera operator emerged. With the advent of artificial lighting and faster (more light sensitive) film stocks, in addition to technological advancements in optics and new techniques such as colour film and widescreen, the technical aspects of cinematography necessitated a specialist in that area.

It was a key during the silent movie era – no sound apart from background music, no dialogue – the films depended on lighting, acting and set.

In **1919**, in **Hollywood**, the *new motion picture capital of the world*, one of the first (and still existing) trade societies was formed: the *American Society of Cinematographers (ASC)*, which stood to recognise the cinematographer's contribution to the art and science of motion picture-making. Similar trade associations have been established in other countries, too.

Quick Facts

- Films are cultural artifacts created by specific cultures, which reflect those cultures, and, in turn, affect them. Film is considered to be an important art form, a source of popular entertainment and a powerful method of educating the people.

- The visual elements of cinema give motion pictures a universal power of communication. Some films have become popular worldwide attractions by using dubbing or subtitles that translate the dialogue into the language of the viewer.

- Films are made up of a series of individual images called frames. When these images are shown rapidly in succession, a viewer has the illusion that motion is occurring. The viewer cannot see the flickering between frames due to an effect known as persistence of vision, whereby the eye retains a visual image for a fraction of a second after the source has been removed. Viewers perceive motion due to a psychological effect called the beta movement.

- CINEMA 4D is a 3D modelling, animation and rendering application developed by MAXON Computer GmbH of Friedrichsdorf, Germany. It is capable of procedural and polygonal/Sub-D modelling, animating, lighting, texturing, rendering and common features found in 3D modelling applications.

Chapter - 8

ELECTRIC BULB

Introduction

Thomas Alva Edison is known as the inventor of the *electric bulb*. But prior to him, many other scientists had been working on manufacturing a reliable source of electric lighting.

An Electric Bulb

In **1800**, **Humphry Davy**, an *English scientist*, made the first electric light. He made an electric battery and to that battery, he attached a piece of carbon with a wire. When the connection was made, the piece of carbon glowed and produced light. It was called an 'electric arc'.

In **1860**, **Sir Joseph Wilson Swan**, an *English physicist*, made an *electric lamp* with a carbon paper filament. It was demonstrated in Newcastle, England. It was not a practical lamp as the filament burnt out very quickly.

An Electric Arc

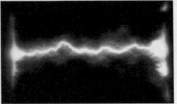

An Electric Arc between Two Metals

Scientists, Inventions and Discoveries

Thomas Alva Edison

Edison, an American inventor, experimented with hundreds of filaments before turning back to the **carbon filament**. In **1879**, he discovered that a carbon filament burns for a long time in vacuum. But it did not last longer than 40 hours. Eventually, he made a carbon filament bulb that could light for over 1500 hours.

Thomas Alva Edison

Working of a Bulb

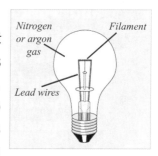

Working of A Bulb

A bulb is a *glass sphere* with a *coiled filament* attached to the base with connecting wires. This filament has a high resistance to electric current. When the current reaches the filament, due to resistance, heat is produced. This heat becomes so much that the filament starts to glow because of it, thus, giving off light.

The most difficult task before Edison was to find a filament which would:

- 💣 Have resistance and glow brightly.
- 💣 Be cheap so that bulbs could be mass produced.
- 💣 Last for a long period of time.

Did You Know?

The shape of a glass bulb was designed by **Matthew Evans** and **Henry Woodward**.

Quick Facts

- Resistance is a property of an element to oppose the flow of current. An element with high resistance towards electric current will give off high amount of heat energy.

- Incandescent bulbs are manufactured in a wide range of sizes, light output and voltage ratings, from 1.5 volts to about 300 volts. They require no external regulating equipment, have low manufacturing costs, and work equally well on either alternating current or direct current. As a result, the incandescent lamp is widely used in household and commercial lighting, for portable lighting, such as table lamps, car headlamps and flashlights, and for decorative and advertising lighting.

- An electric bulb is one of the revolutionary inventions ever made in the history of mankind. The working of an electric bulb is quite simple. When electric current flows through the filament made up of tungsten, it heats up emitting visible light.

Chapter - 9

FOUNTAIN PEN

Introduction

The first practical fountain pen was patented by **Lewis E. Waterman** in the year, **1884**. The first American patent for a pen was received by a shoemaker Peregrin Williamson in 1809. Following this, in 1819, John Scheffer received a British patent for his pen which was half quill and half metal pen.

A Fountain Pen

However, the first *self- filling fountain pen* was patented by **John Jacob Parker** in the year, **1831**. But all these fountain pens had a huge drawback – that of ink spills. This made the mass sale of these fountain pens very low.

Did You Know?

The Fountain Pen made by a Frenchman, M.Bion in the year, *1702 is the oldest pen to survive.*

The early attempts at making a pen were inspired by the working of a *feather quill.*

A Quill Pen

The first quills were made up of bird's feathers. A feather has a hollow channel through which the ink gets sucked up and get stored in it. But it is a natural object and a man-made pen on similar lines was incapable of holding the ink for long. A long, thin rubber reservoir attached to a metal nib and filled with ink was not a good option.

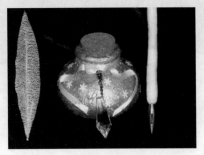

A Metal Nib Quill

Also, Lewis Waterman, who was an insurance salesman, had to cancel an important sales contact with leaky pens to start work on improving his fountain pen.

Mechanism of a Fountain Pen

A fountain pen has three parts: a nib, a feed (black part under the nib) and a barrel. The nib comes in contact with paper. The feed regulates the flow of ink from the reservoir to the nib. The round barrel, holding the nib and feed on the writing end encases the ink reservoir. **Lewis Waterman** thought of adding an air hole in the nib and three grooves inside the feed.

Fountain pens have an internal reservoir of ink. Different pens had different concepts of filling the reservoirs. Earlier pens used droppers to fill ink. By **1915**, most pens were equipped with *self-filling ink reservoirs* made of rubber. The reservoirs were squeezed flat and then the nib was inserted in the ink bottle. The pressure on the reservoir was released and the nib would then suck up the ink to fill the empty reservoir.

Quick Facts

- The fountain pen's design came after a thousand years of using quill-pens. Several different patents issued for the self-filling fountain pen design are: The Button Filler: Patented in 1905 and first offered by the Parker Pen Co. in 1913 as an alternative to the eyedropper method, it is an external button connected to the internal pressure plate that flattened the ink sac when pressed.

- The Lever Filler: Walter Sheaffer patented the lever filler in 1908. The W.A. Sheaffer Pen Company of Fort Madison, Iowa introduced it in 1912. An external lever depressed the flexible ink sac. The lever fitted flush with the barrel of the pen when it was not in use. The lever filler became the winning design for the next forty years, the button filler coming in second.

- The Click Filler: First called the crescent filler, Roy Conklin of Toledo commercially produced the first one. A later design by Parker Pen Co. used the name click filler. When two protruding tabs on the outside of the pen pressed, the ink sac deflated. The tabs would make a clicking sound when the sac was full.

- The Matchstick Filler: Introduced around 1910 by the Weidlich Company, it is a small rod mounted on the pen or a common matchstick depressed the internal pressure plate through a hole in the side of the barrel.

- The Coin Filler: Developed by Lewis Waterman in an attempt to compete with the winning lever filler patent belonging to Sheaffer, it is a slot in the barrel of the pen enabled a coin to deflate the internal pressure plate, a similar idea to the matchstick filler.

Chapter - 10

PRINTING PRESS

Introduction

The invention of printing press is the most revolutionary aspect of *modern mass communication*. The world of print communication is solely depended on the printing press.

Modern Printing Press

A printing press is a device used for inking the surface of the paper with a set pattern, usually text, by applying pressure on the paper surface.

A printing press is used to *publish books, magazines, newspapers, leaflets, brochures, posters* and other *literature*.

Johannes Gutenberg's Printing Press

The world's first printing press was set up by Johannes Gutenberg in the year **1440**. He was a *German goldsmith*, who along with **Andreas Dritzehn** and **Andreas Heilmann** started the printing press. Dritzehn was a gem cutter and Heilmann was the owner of a paper mill. With the help of his knowledge of metals, Gutenberg started making movable metal/ wooden letters type blocks. By 1436, he had made type blocks to be used in his printing press.

Gutenberg's printing press was a hand press on which a wooden form held together the raised hand set block letters. The ink was poured over on this wooden form and this was then pressed against the sheet of paper.

Johannes Gutenberg

Did You Know?

Johannes Gutenberg printed *world's first book using movable type printing press*. It was a **42 line (42 words per page) Bible**. It is called **Gutenberg's Bible**.

Working of a Printing Press

A printing press is made up of different sizes and types of rollers attached to it. Ink is poured over the first roller so that it spreads evenly on the whole surface and covers the area evenly. After the ink is rolled on the cylinders, the colour is transferred to the cylinder which contains the text or image plate. This roller turns in a periodic manner at exact same rotation speed. The text/image are transferred to a blanket cylinder. A sheet of paper is inserted between this blanket cylinder and impression cylinder. All these cylinders rotate simultaneously in a similar manner to get a good print.

Gutenberg's Printing Press

Working Printing Press

Quick Facts

🗣 During the centuries, many newer printing technologies were developed based on Gutenberg's printing machine e.g. the offset printing.

🗣 Gutenberg began experimenting with metal typography (Letterpress Printing) after he had moved from his native town of Mainz to Strassburg around 1430. Gutenberg concluded that metal type could be reproduced much more quickly once a single mould had been fashioned.

🗣 The Diamond Sutra, a Buddhist scripture, was the first dated example of block printing.

🗣 Gutenberg completed his wooden press which used movable metal type.

🗣 The first known colour printing came out of a Psalter (a collection of Psalms for devotional use) by Faust in 1457.

🗣 Two hundred woodcuts were used in an edition of Aesop's Fables.

🗣 The first use of copper engravings instead of woodcuts for illustration was made in 1476.

🗣 Printing had become established in more than 2500 cities around Europe by the year, 1499.

Chapter - 11

TELEVISION

Introduction

Television is a *medium of mass communication*. It is a device which *receives* and *transmits* moving images *(audio and video)*. Television is the most important medium of **electronic communication**.

A Modern Television

The word, television is made up of two words – 'tele' (Greek word) meaning far and 'visio' (Latin word) meaning sight. Thus, the word, television means 'far sight'.

John Logie Baird

The invention of *television* cannot be credited to a single person. Many people have worked towards its development. However, John Logie Baird is considered to be the person responsible for the invention of television. Prior to Baird, many inventions were made based on whom he set up his television design. **Ferdinand Braun**, in the year **1897**, invented the **cathode ray**

John Logie Baird

tube which is the most important element of a television setup. In the year 1907, the cathode ray tube was first used to produce television images.

He is credited for being the first person to produce a *live and moving greyscale image* from reflected light. In 1923-1924, he made the *world's first working television set* using things like old hatbox, scissors, sewing needles, bicycle lenses, sealing wax and glue!

Did You Know?

John Baird *survived a 1000 volt electric shock* while working on his experiment.

Baird transmitted the world's first long-distance television pictures to the Central Hotel at Glasgow Central Station in the year 1927.

He set up the Baird Television Development Company Ltd in 1928. Through this company, he made the first transatlantic television transmission, from London to New York.

An Early Television

Working of a Television

The data (audio-video) is converted into electric signal. This electric signal is then transmitted through a transmitter into the atmosphere.

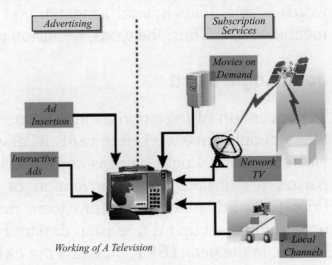

Working of A Television

These signals are then received by an antenna which converts them back into audio and video data. This data is then seen and heard on the television screen.

Philo Farnsworth

Quick Facts

- In 1938, the television broadcasts were, for the first time, able to be taped and edited. Prior to that, only live transmission was possible.

- Philo Farnsworth (Great Britain) transmitted the television image in 1927.

- In 1960 roughly 100 million television sets were sold worldwide and in 1962, the first satellite TV transmission took place between France and the United States.

- The first television transmission from the moon took place in 1969.

- In 1997, the DVD player was introduced at the Consumer Electronics Show.

- In 2005, the Flat-panel high-definition televisions became the "must have" product of the year. The Sling box product used the Internet to stream your local television anywhere in the world you've got a high speed Internet connection.

Chapter - 12

TRANSFORMER

Introduction

A transformer is an *electronic device* which is used to *transfer electric current from one circuit to another*.

A Transformer

Did You Know?

The electricity you get in your house comes to you through a *big transformer*. The *electricity board* transmits *electric current* through *wires* to a *transformer* in your residential area. This transformer then distributes the electricity to each and every house of the area. If there was no transformer, the electric current coming straight from electricity board to your house would be very high and would destroy the electric circuit in your house. Then you won't be able to run a tube light or a fan.

William Stanley

Though the *principle of induction* was discovered in as early as **1830**, William Stanley built the first advanced, commercially used transformer in the year, **1886**. However, the first transformer was invented by **Ottó**

Bláthy, Miksa Déri and **Károly Zipernowsky** of the Austro-Hungarian Empire.

His transformer was based on the basic designs by the *Ganz Company in Hungary (ZBD Transformer 1878)* and *Lucien Gaulard* and *John Dixon Gibbs in England. Gaulard and Gibbs* started the first work on transformers while Stanley made the transformer cheap to produce and easy to use.

William Stanley

Construction of a Transformer

A transformer is a device made up of an *insulated metal core* (usually iron). The two parallel arms of the iron core are coiled with copper wires. These two coils are called *primary and secondary winding.*

Working of a Transformer

The primary winding of the transformer gets the input voltage which is converted from *low voltage to high voltage or vice-versa.* To convert low voltage to high voltage, the coils in the secondary windings are increased. To convert high voltage to low voltage, the coils in the secondary windings are decreased.

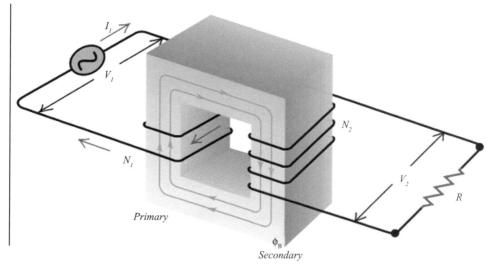
Working of a Transformer

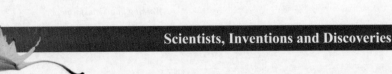

Chapter - 13

STEAM ENGINE

Introduction

A steam engine is an engine which performs **mechanical work** using *steam* as its driving force. Though very scarcely put to use today, steam engines were a revolutionary invention and is considered as one of the greatest achievements of the modern world.

A Steam Locomotive

James Watt

Although **James Watt** is credited as the inventor of Steam Engine, *Thomas Savery* and *Thomas Newcomen* were two inventors who designed the crude and very basic steam engine.

Thomas Savery, an English military engineer, was the first to patent the basic crude steam engine in **1698**, based on the designs of *Denis Papin's pressure cooker*. Thomas Newcomen

James Watt

later improved upon Savery's design. But it was *Scotsman James Watt's* improved design which helped in ushering a new era of **Industrial Revolution**.

Did You Know?

James Watt coined the term, **'horsepower'** as a way to help explain how much work his steam engines could do for a potential buyer.

In 1765, James Watt, *a professor in the University of Glasgow*, was asked to work on improving the workability of Newcomen's steam engine. He attached a *separate condenser* connected to a *cylinder by a valve*. This design became very popular as it was workable and thus, James Watt is regarded as the inventor of a commercially useful steam engine.

Working of a Steam Engine

A steam engine is equipped with a *heating furnace* and a *water boiler. Coal* is used to burn the furnace and give huge amount of heat. This heat turns the water in the boiler into steam. This steam after reaching high pressure is passed through pistons and turbines. When these pistons and turbines expand, they move, and along with it moves the shaft, which at one end is attached to the wheels. This way, the heat energy is converted into mechanical energy.

Basically, a steam engine is able to *harness the energy of steam to move machinery*. It is a fairly clean source of energy. Steam engines were used to a great effect to *run locomotives and steamships*.

Quick Facts

- Industrial Revolution was the era from 1750–1850 in which many industrial reforms took place; Steam Engine is one of them.

- Steam engines are still used today to help run nuclear power plants.

- The Watt – a unit of power used today with lightbulbs – was named after James Watt.

- James Watt came up with the term, 'horsepower' as a way to help explain how much work his steam engines could do for a potential buyer.

- The first loco to hit 100 mph (160 km/h) was in the City of Truro in 1895.

- The Flying Scotsman was a famous loco designed by Sir Nigel Gresley (1876-1941). It pulled trains non-stop in the 630 km stretch from London to Edinhurgli in less than six hours.

- Coal and water are often stored in a wagon called a tender, towed behind the locomotive. A tender holds 10 tons of coal and 30,000 litres of water.

Chapter - 14

TELEPHONE

Introduction

The word, telephone is made up of two words, 'tele' meaning distance and 'phonetics' meaning sound. Thus, Telephone means *sound from a distance.*

Telephone

In the beginning, there was only one kind of telephone – *a fixed cable handset with a receiver and a body with a dial pad.* It is known as **'Landline'** today. As the technology progressed, a new kind of phone came into being – **a cordless phone**.

Did You Know?

Alexander Graham Bell was the first person to invent a telephone, in the year, **1876**.

George Sweigert

George Sweigert, in **1966**, invented the *cordless phone – a portable phone without a cable.* It consisted of a handset with speaker/ receiver and a

George Sweigert

base station. This phone could be carried around within a specified range of the base station. This provided tremendous flexibility to the user. The only drawback was that it needed to be plugged into the base for charging.

Then in 1973, **Dr. Martin Cooper of Motorola** came out with the first mobile phone of the history. This is hailed as one of the *biggest revolution in the field of telecommunication*. Today, almost every person carries a **mobile phone**.

Dr. Martin Cooper

Alexander Graham Bell

He made *his first telephone* on **June 2, 1875** and at the age of 29, Bell presented his first 'telephone' to the world in the year, 1876. In 1877, he formed the **Bell Telephone Company**. Throughout his life, Bell worked for the betterment of the *deaf and mute people*. His mother lost her hearing ability later in life. This led Bell to research and invent various means of communication for such people. This interest led him to invent the **'microphone'** which formed the basis for his **'electrical speech machine'**. This machine was what we know today as telephone.

Alexander Graham Bell

By 1878, Bell had set up the *first telephone exchange* in New Haven, Connecticut. By 1884, long distance connections were made between Boston, Massachusetts and New York City.

Working Components of a Telephone

As it has since its early years, the telephone instrument is made up of the following functional components: a power source, a switch hook, a dialler, a ringer, a transmitter, a receiver, and an anti-sidetone circuit.

In the first experimental telephones, the electric current that powered the telephone circuit was generated at the transmitter, by means of an electromagnet activated by the speaker's voice. Such a system could not generate enough voltage to produce audible speech. So every transmitter since Bell's patented design has operated on a direct current supplied by an independent power source. The first sources were batteries located in the telephone instruments themselves, but since the 1890s, the current has been generated at the local switching office. The current is supplied through a two-wire circuit called the local loop. The standard voltage is 48 volts.

Switch Hook

The switch hook connects the telephone instrument to the direct current supplied through the local loop. In early telephones, the receiver was hung on a hook that operated the switch by opening and closing a metal contact. This system is still common, though the hook has been replaced by a cradle to hold the combined handset, enclosing both the receiver and the transmitter. In some modern electronic instruments, the mechanical operation of metal contacts has been replaced by a system of transistor relays.

Switch Hook

When the telephone is 'on hook,' contact with the local loop is broken. When it is 'off hook' (i.e., when the handset is lifted from the cradle), contact is restored, and the current flows through the loop. The switching office signals restoration of contact by transmitting a low-frequency 'dial tone' — actually two simultaneous tones of 350 and 440 Hertz.

Dialler

The dialler is used to enter the number of the party that the user wishes to call. Signals generated by the dialer activate switches in the local office, which establish a transmission path to the called party. Dialers are of the rotary and push-button types.

Push Button Dialer

The traditional rotary dialler, invented in the 1890s, is rotated against the tension of a spring and then released, whereupon it returns to its position at a rate controlled by a mechanical governor. The return rotation causes a switch to open and close, producing interruptions, or pulses, in the flow of direct current to the switching office. Each pulse lasts approximately one-tenth of a second; the number of pulses signals the number being dialled.

In push-button dialling, introduced in the 1960s, the pressing of each button generates a 'dual-tone' signal that is specific to the number being entered. Each dual tone is composed of a low frequency (697, 770, 852, or 941 hertz) and a high frequency (1,209, 1,336, or 1,477 hertz), which are sensed and decoded at the switching office. Unlike the low-frequency rotary pulses, dual tones can travel through the telephone system, so that push-button telephones can be used to activate automated functions at the other end of the line.

In both rotary and push-button systems, a capacitor and resistor prevent dialling signals from passing into the ringer circuit.

Ringer

The ringer alerts the user to an incoming call by emitting an audible tone or ring. Ringers are of two types, mechanical or electronic. Both types are activated by a 20-hertz, 75-volt alternating current generated by the switching office. The ringer is

Ringer

activated in two-second pulses, each pulse separated by a pause of four seconds.

The traditional mechanical ringer was introduced with the early Bell telephones. It consists of two closely spaced bells, a metal clapper, and a magnet. Passage of alternating current through a coil of wire produces alternations in the magnetic attraction exerted on the clapper, so that it vibrates rapidly and loudly against the bells. Volume can be muted by a switch that places a mechanical damper against the bells.

In modern electronic ringers, introduced in the 1980s, the ringer current is passed through an oscillator, which adjusts the current to the precise frequency required to activate a piezoelectric transducer—a device made of a crystalline material that vibrates in response to an electric current. The transducer may be coupled to a small loudspeaker, which can be adjusted for volume.

The ringer circuit remains connected to the local loop even when the telephone is on hook. A larger voltage is necessary to activate the ringer. A capacitor prevents direct current from passing through the ringer once the handset has been lifted off the switch hook.

Transmitter

The transmitter is essentially a tiny microphone located in the mouthpiece of the telephone's handset. It converts vibrations of the speaker's voice into variations in the direct current flowing through the set from the power source.

In modern electric transmitters, developed in the 1970s, the carbon layer is replaced by a thin plastic sheet that has been given a conductive metallic coating on one side. The plastic separates that coating from another metal electrode and maintains an electric field between them. Vibrations caused

Transmitter

  **Scientists, Inventions and Discoveries**

by speech produce fluctuations in the electric field, which in turn produce small variations in voltage. The voltages are amplified for transmission over the telephone line.

Receiver

The receiver is located in the earpiece of the telephone's handset. Operating on electromagnetic principles that were known in Bell's day, the receiver converts fluctuating *electric current into sound waves that reproduce human speech*. Fundamentally, it consists of two parts: a permanent magnet, having pole pieces wound with coils of insulated fine wire, and a diaphragm driven by magnetic material that is supported near the pole pieces.

Receiver

Anti-sidetone Circuit

The anti-sidetone circuit is an assemblage of *transformers, resistors, and capacitors* that perform a number of functions. The primary function is to reduce the sidetone, which is the distracting sound of the speaker's own voice coming through the receiver from the transmitter.

The *anti-sidetone circuit* accomplishes this reduction by interposing a transformer between the transmitter circuit and the receiver circuit and by splitting the transmitter signals along two paths. When the divided signals, having opposite polarities, meet at the transformer, they almost entirely cancel each other in crossing to the receiver circuit. The speech signal coming from the other end of the line, on the other hand, arrives at the transformer along a single, undivided path and crosses the transformer undisturbed.

Anti-sidetone Circuit

Working of a Telephone

A telephone consists of a microphone which converts the sound waves into electric current and sends it through a telephone network to another phone. The earphone or speaker in the receiving phone converts this electric signal back into sound wave.

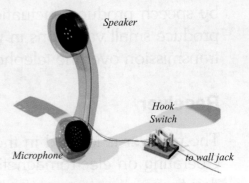

Working of a Telephone

Quick Facts

- The telephone network extends worldwide, so you can reach nearly anyone on the planet.

- Alexander Graham Bell experimented with his "harmonic telegraph" for two years before getting it patented by the U.S. Patent Office. On March 10, 1876 he was able to get his phone to work.

- The first words spoken through a telephone were "Watson come here, I want you!" The phone call was made by Alexander Graham Bell to his assistant, Thomas A. Watson.

- Mark Twain was one of the first people to have a phone in his home.

- Alexander Graham Bell also invented the metal detector.

- When Alexander Graham Bell died in 1922, all telephones stopped from ringing for one full minute as a tribute to the creator.

- The first transatlantic telephone cable was used in 1956. A telephone cable was run across the ocean floor and lies as deep as 12,000 feet. The cable runs across the Atlantic Ocean from Canada to Scotland.

Chapter - 15

ELECTRIC MOTOR

Introduction

An electric motor is a device which turns or converts *electrical energy* into *mechanical energy*.

An Electric Motor

Electric motors are found in many appliances, ranging from small devices like electric wrist watch, pump, geyser, blower, mixer-juicer, to bigger appliances like fans, air conditioners, coolers, industrial mills.

Electric motors of high efficiency were started being made from 1821. However, the first commercially successful motor was made in 1873. The working of an electric motor is based on **Faraday's law of induction**.

Nikola Tesla

Nikola Tesla made the first **Alternating Current** or **AC Motor** in the year, 1888. AC or Alternate Current Motor was an admirable step towards highly efficient and less heat-generating motor advancement. Prior to that, in the year **1886**, **Frank Julian Sprague**

Nikola Tesla

had made a DC or Direct Current Motor. The AC motors had an advantage over DC motors as the former provided high efficiency and could run most of the appliances without conversion.

Today, only Alternating Current or AC motors are mostly used because AC is the general form in which electricity is carried to homes, offices, businesses, industries.

Working of an Electric Motor

A simple motor consists of the following six parts – *rotor, commutator, brushes, axle, field magnet* and *power supply.*

The field magnet is a **permanent magnet**. The **wire coil** is wrapped around an **armature**. The wire coil is attached to a source of current. When the electric current flows through the wire coil, a **magnetic field** develops around the armature. Thus, the armature behaves like an **electromagnet**. Now the field

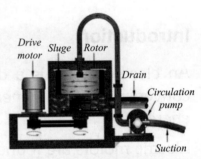

Working of a Electric Motor

magnet attracts and repels the magnetised armature. This makes the armature move a full rotation. This armature is attached with a shaft at one end with the help of an axle. When the axle moves because of repeated rotation of the armature, mechanical energy is produced. Thus, the *electrical energy* is converted into *mechanical energy.*

Quick Facts

- Michael Faraday's law of induction states the relationship between the production of mechanical force by the interaction of electric current and magnetic field.

- Most electric motors operate through the interaction of magnetic fields and current-carrying conductors to generate force.

- Electric motors and generators are commonly referred to as electric machines. They may be powered by direct current, e.g., a battery powered portable device or motor vehicle, or by alternating current from a central electrical distribution grid or inverter.

- The smallest motors may be found in electric wristwatches.

Exercises

I. Answer the following questions.

1. Who was Archimedes and what was he famous for?

2. State and explain the Archimedes Principle briefly.

3. Explain the Archimedes Heat Rays with the help of a diagram.

4. What do you understand by the claw of Archimedes? Explain with the help of a diagram.

5. What does Archimedes explain in his books, *On the Equilibrium of Planes* (two volumes)?

6. Explain the method of exhaustion as devised by Archimedes.

7. Who was Alexander Graham Bell and what is he famous for?

8. Give a detailed account of the inventions and discoveries of Alexander Graham Bell right from the age of 12.

9. Who was Albert Einstein and what is he famous for?

10. Explain the discoveries and inventions of Einstein briefly.

II. Fill in the blanks with suitable words.

1. Benjamin Franklin was a celebrated American scientist, _____ and _____.

2. Benjamin Franklin was the one to discover the _____.

3. Franklin also gave the world, _____ , i.e., spectacles with two lenses in each frame so that a person could use the same spectacle for watching near and far things at the same time.

4. _____ is famously remembered for his scientific theory of evolution named 'Natural Selection'.

5. _____ was an Italian mathematician, astronomer, physicist and philosopher.

6. At the age of 21, Galileo discovered the_____.

7. _____ is remembered for his invention of film roll.

8. George Eastman founded the famous _____ in Rochester, New York in the year, 1892.

9. Sir Isaac Newton is famous for his _____ and the concept of _____.

10. The French chemist and microbiologist, _____ created the first vaccines for rabies and anthrax.

III. Match the two columns correctly.

A	B
1. Micro-organisms are very tiny organisms	we have electric bulbs in our homes.
2. The SI unit of capacitance is named 'Farad'	that harm living beings by attacking any weak spot in their bodies.
3. Thomas Edison is the reason	to honour the contribution of Michael Faraday.
4. Faraday was mainly a chemist. In 1825,	Indian-American astrophysicist.
5. Subrahmanyan Chandrasekhar was an eminent	he discovered the important chemical, Benzene.

IV. Multiple Choice Questions (MCQs)

1. Marie Curie is the first scientist to win two Nobel Prizes, one in Physics and the other in _____.

   a. Biology   b. Chemistry   c. Astrophysics

2. Radium was named so because of its intense radioactivity and Polonium was named so after the birth land, _____ of Madam Curie.

   a. Poland   b. Finland   c. Greenland

3. Thomas Alva Edison set up the world's first electric light power station in Lower Manhattan, but he was _____.

   a. Dumb   b. Blind   c. Deaf

4. S. Chandrasekhar was awarded the Nobel Prize for Physics and also the _____.

   a. Padma Vibhushan   b. Bharat Ratna

   c. Padma Shri

5. Sir J.C. Bose is well reputed for his contribution towards plant science and his research work in the field of _____.

   a. Electromagnetic waves

   b. Radio and microwave optics

   c. Electricity

6. India celebrates the *National Science Day* on *February 28* of every year to commemorate the discovery of the _____.

   a. Bose Effect   b. Doppler Effect

   c. Raman Effect

7. Bacteria were first found by_____ in the year, 1667.

    a. Louis Pasteur   b. Antonie Van Leeuwenhoek

    c. Charles Darwin

8. Bacteria are used to clean water in sewage plants, and they produce _____.

    a. Oxygen   b. Nitrogen   c. Hydrogen

9. Vitamins are classified as either water-soluble or fat-soluble. In humans, there are _____.

    a. 10 vitamins   b. 12 vitamins   c. 13 vitamins

10. Most human cases of rabies are due to transmission of the virus through _____.

    a. Cat bites   b. Dog bites   c. Livestock

Glossary

Astronomer: A scientific observer of celestial bodies

Philosopher: A person who is deeply versed in philosophy

Inclination: Bent, a disposition

Premature: Immature, mature or ripe before proper time

Maternal: Related through mother

Enrolled: Enlisted, to put in record

Electrolysis: The conduction of electricity by a solution

Knighted: A man upon whom is the non-hereditary dignity of knighthood (honour)

Experiences: Process or act of personally encountering

Wonder: To think or speculate curiously

Proposed: To suggest, offer

Accurate: Exact, precise

Microbiologist: A branch of Biology which deals with the structure and function of micro-organisms

Rabies: An infectious disease of dogs or cats transmitted by bite to human beings

Anthrax: An infectious, often fatal disease of cattle, sheep, etc.

Souring: Having an acid taste, fermented

Sanitize: Sterilize, make free from dirt, germs, etc.

Gadgets: Mechanical devices

Immune: Protected or exempted from a disease

Prestigious: Honourable, having a high reputation

Sterilization: Disinfected, making germ-free

Superseded: To succeed to the position in power

Exploration: Investigation

Properties: Qualities, features

Emitted: Discharged, reflected

Eradicate: To remove or destroy completely

Tumour: A swollen part, protuberance

Unaware: Not aware or conscious, unconscious

Supplement: Something added to complete a thing

Phonograph: Any sound-reproducing-machine

Filament: A very fine threadlike structure

Incandescent: Glowing or white with heat, brilliant

Complications: Confusions, a complex combination of events

Inspiration: A divine influence

Perspiration: Sweating, the act of eliminating fluid through the pores of the skin

Intellectual: A person of superior intelligence

Attainments: Accomplishments, Achievements

Pivotal: Vital, very important

Evolve: Develop gradually

Eminent: Prominent, noteworthy, distinguished, reputed

Immense: Vast, huge, very great

Variations: Amount, rate, extent or degree of change

Stagnated: Still and become stale

Amidst: Within, surrounding

Harsh: Unpleasant

All ▾

Hello, Sign in
Account & Lists ▾

Returns
& Orders ▾

Try
Prime ▾

Cart

Hello
Select your address

Mobiles | Best Sellers | Today's Deals | Computers | Pantry | Books | Gift Ideas | New Releases | Customer Service | Amazon Pay | Sell | Baby | AmazonBasics | Coupons

THE GEN X SERIES

V&S PUBLISHERS

VALUE & SUBSTANCE

HOME   EBOOKS   BEST SELLERS   ACADEMIC BOOKS   CHILDREN BOOKS   HINDI   ENGLISH IMPROVEMENT   REGIONAL BOOKS   COMBO PACKS ▾

V&S PUBLISHERS

RAPIDEX COURSES → RELIGION

OLYMPIADS   CHILDREN STORIES

ENGLISH IMPROVEMENT   SELF HELP

DICTIONARIES   SCHOOL BOOKS

CRAFT & HOBBY   HEALTH

ACADEMIC   GENERAL KNOWLEDGE

E-books

Bestsellers
Subjects   Olympiads

Publishers of Olympiads
School Books & General Books

V&S PUBLISHERS	
EBOOKS	›
BEST SELLERS	
ACADEMIC BOOKS	›
CHILDREN BOOKS	›
HINDI	
ENGLISH IMPROVEMENT	›
REGIONAL BOOKS	
COMBO PACKS	
STUDENT DEVELOPMENT	›
COMPUTER & IT	
WOMEN ORIENTED	›
FAMILY & RELATIONSHIP	
SELF HELP	›
HEALTH & FITNESS	›
RELIGION & SPIRITUALITY	›
LEISURE & LIFESTYLE	›

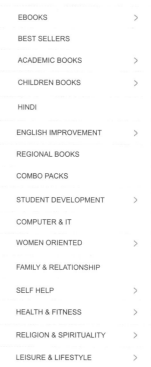

Why Should You Read Our Books?

Published by Top Brand
V&S Publishers is a Leading National Level Publisher for Academic & General Books with over 1000 titles published across 50 categories in 10 languages. All books are available as Ebooks on Kindle Worldwide besides being sold as paperbacks through big and small bookstores pan India.

Written by Experts
Each Book is perfectly crafted by Subject Matter Experts & uniquely designed in-house. It offers a rich blended learning & reading experience through simple, quality & informative content. All books are thoroughly edited by experienced editors for grammar, language & factual error.

Assured Production Quality
Production Analysts with decades of experience hand-pick thick, high-quality paper for every book. Each book is machine bound and printed using non-toxic ink at high-end imported printing presses. All books are packaged and singly shrink-wrapped for protection from dust and damage.

On-time Delivery
Each product is exclusively sold by reputed prime sellers & is double-checked for new condition & best in-class packaging standards before despatch. To ensure on-time & rightful delivery, premier courier partners only are chosen for deliveries across all cities.

Buy All Books Online From Our Amazon Brandstore:
amazon.in/vspublishers

➤ All V&S Publishers' books are available at best discounts with COD facility on Amazon, Flipkart & Snapdeal.
➤ Search all books by their ISBNs.

➤ अब 'वी एण्ड एस पब्लिशर्स' की सभी लोकप्रिय पुस्तकें COD सुविधा द्वारा Amazon, Flipkart & Snapdeal पर उपलब्ध।
➤ पुस्तक की खरीद के लिए ISBNs नंबर सर्च करें।

Head Office: F-2/16, Ansari Road, Daryaganj, New Delhi-110002, Ph: 011-23240026/27/28 Email: sales@vspublishers.com
Regional Office: 5-1-707/1, Brij Bhawan (Beside Central Bank of India Lane) Bank Street, Koti, Hyderabad-500 095
Ph: 040-24737290 Email: vspublishershyd@gmail.com

V&S OLYMPIAD GUIDE BOOK AND WORKBOOK SERIES (CLASSES 1-10)

ISBN : 9789357940504	ISBN : 9789357942447
ISBN : 9789357940511	ISBN : 9789357942454
ISBN : 9789357940528	ISBN : 9789357942461
ISBN : 9789357940535	ISBN : 9789357942478
ISBN : 9789357940542	ISBN : 9789357942

ISBN : 9789357940559	ISBN : 9789357942492
ISBN : 9789357940566	ISBN : 9789357942508
ISBN : 9789357940573	ISBN : 9789357942515
ISBN : 9789357940580	ISBN : 9789357942522
ISBN : 9789357940597	ISBN : 9789357942

ISBN : 9789357940405	ISBN : 9789357942546
ISBN : 9789357940412	ISBN : 9789357942553
ISBN : 9789357940429	ISBN : 9789357942560
ISBN : 9789357940436	ISBN : 9789357942577
ISBN : 9789357940443	ISBN : 9789357942

ISBN : 9789357940450	ISBN : 9789357942591
ISBN : 9789357940467	ISBN : 9789357942607
ISBN : 9789357940474	ISBN : 9789357942614
ISBN : 9789357940481	ISBN : 9789357942621
ISBN : 9789357940498	ISBN : 9789357942

ISBN : 9789357942102	ISBN : 9789357942744
ISBN : 9789357940603	ISBN : 9789357942751
ISBN : 9789357940610	ISBN : 9789357942768
ISBN : 9789357940627	ISBN : 9789357942775
ISBN : 9789357940634	ISBN : 9789357942

ISBN : 9789357940641	ISBN : 9789357942799
ISBN : 9789357940658	ISBN : 9789357942805
ISBN : 9789357940665	ISBN : 9789357942812
ISBN : 9789357940672	ISBN : 9789357942829
ISBN : 9789357940689	ISBN : 9789357942

ISBN : 9789357940696	ISBN : 9789357942645
ISBN : 9789357940702	ISBN : 9789357942652
ISBN : 9789357940719	ISBN : 9789357942669
ISBN : 9789357940726	ISBN : 9789357942676
ISBN : 9789357940733	ISBN : 9789357942

ISBN : 9789357940740	ISBN : 9789357942690
ISBN : 9789357940757	ISBN : 9789357942706
ISBN : 9789357940764	ISBN : 9789357942713
ISBN : 9789357940771	ISBN : 9789357942720
ISBN : 9789357940788	ISBN : 9789357942

ISBN : 9789357942263	ISBN : 9789357942003
ISBN : 9789357942270	ISBN : 9789357942010
ISBN : 9789357942287	ISBN : 9789357942027
ISBN : 9789357942294	ISBN : 9789357942034
ISBN : 9789357942300	ISBN : 9789357

ISBN : 9789357942317	ISBN : 9789357942058
ISBN : 9789357942324	ISBN : 9789357942065
ISBN : 9789357942331	ISBN : 9789357942072
ISBN : 9789357942348	ISBN : 9789357942089
ISBN : 9789357942355	ISBN : 9789357

CAREER & BUSINESS/SELF-HELP/PERSONALITY DEVELOPMENT/STRESS MANAGEMENT

ISBN : 9789381588789 ISBN : 9789350571637 ISBN : 9789381588512 ISBN : 9789381588963 ISBN : 9789381588598 ISBN : 9789381384039 ISBN : 9788192079622 ISBN : 9789350570753 ISBN : 9789381384396

ISBN : 9789357940115 ISBN : 9789350570968 ISBN : 9789381384527 ISBN : 9789381588666 ISBN : 9789381384541 ISBN : 9789381384107 ISBN : 9789350571187 ISBN : 9789381588574 ISBN : 9789381588277

ISBN : 9789381588222 ISBN : 9789381384213 ISBN : 9789381588772 ISBN : 9789381588949 ISBN : 9789357940108 ISBN : 9789381384152 ISBN : 9789381384145 ISBN : 9789381448564 ISBN : 9789381384473

ISBN : 9789381448595 ISBN : 9789381448670 ISBN : 9789381588253 ISBN : 9789381448755 ISBN : 9789381448649 ISBN : 9789381384480 ISBN : 9789350571309 ISBN : 9789381448632 ISBN : 9789381384893

ISBN : 9789381384091 ISBN : 9789381384176 ISBN : 9789350570265 ISBN : 9789381588727 ISBN : 9789381384411 ISBN : 9789381588246 ISBN : 9789381448687 ISBN : 9789381448786 ISBN : 9789381448533

ISBN : 9789381448526 ISBN : 9789381384206 ISBN : 9788122310689 ISBN : 9789381384503 ISBN : 9789381588505 ISBN : 9789381448717 ISBN : 9788192079646 ISBN : 9789350570203 ISBN : 9789350570272

ISBN : 9789381588741 ISBN : 9789350571170 ISBN : 9789381588215 ISBN : 9789381384763 ISBN : 9789350570296 ISBN : 9789381588284 ISBN : 9789381588543 ISBN : 9789350571880 ISBN : 9789381588765

ISBN : 9789350570579 ISBN : 9789350571927 ISBN : 9789350571545 ISBN : 9789381384114 ISBN : 9789381384435 ISBN : 9789381448779 ISBN : 9789381448991 ISBN : 9789381384510 ISBN : 9789381384169 ISBN : 9789350570623

ISBN : 9789381448908 ISBN : 9789381448915 ISBN : 9789381448922 ISBN : 9789381448939 ISBN : 9789381448946 ISBN : 9789357940795 ISBN : 9789357940801 ISBN : 9789357940818 ISBN : 9789357941303 ISBN : 9789357941853

STUDENT LEARNING/QUIZ/POPULAR SCIENCE/BIOGRAPHIES

ISBN : 9789357941310 ISBN : 9789357941495 ISBN : 9789357942430 ISBN : 9789381384053 ISBN : 9789381384060 ISBN : 9789381384121 ISBN : 9788122310924 ISBN : 9789381588468 ISBN : 9789381588604 ISBN : 9789350570494

ISBN : 9789350570470 ISBN : 9789350570487 ISBN : 9789350570500 ISBN : 9789350570586 ISBN : 9789350571248 ISBN : 9789350571248 ISBN : 9789350571743 ISBN : 9789381384299 ISBN : 9789381448052

ISBN : 9789381384305 ISBN : 9789381384954 ISBN : 9789381588819 ISBN : 9789350570371 ISBN : 9789350570388 ISBN : 9789350570395 ISBN : 9789350570401 ISBN : 9789350570364 ISBN : 9789381588444

ISBN : 9789381448977 ISBN : 9789381384459 ISBN : 9789381384930 ISBN : 9789350571682 ISBN : 9789381588864 ISBN : 9789381588673 ISBN : 9789350570111 ISBN : 9789381384312 ISBN : 9789381588680

ISBN : 9789350570258 ISBN : 9789350570227 ISBN : 9789381588499 ISBN : 9789381588338 ISBN : 9789381588345 ISBN : 9789381448656 ISBN : 9789381384558 ISBN : 9788192079639 ISBN : 9789350571019

ISBN : 9789350571026 ISBN : 9789350571033 ISBN : 9789350571040 ISBN : 9789350571057 ISBN : 9789350570999 ISBN : 9789350571002 ISBN : 9789350571064 ISBN : 9789350571071 ISBN : 9789350571088

ISBN : 9789350571101 ISBN : 9789381588321 ISBN : 9789381588307 ISBN : 9789381588567 ISBN : 9789350571163 ISBN : 9789350570517 ISBN : 9789381384183 ISBN : 9789381448625 ISBN : 9789381384794

ISBN : 9789381384190 ISBN : 9789381448793 ISBN : 9789381588192 ISBN : 9789381588802 ISBN : 9789381588970 ISBN : 9789350570777 ISBN : 9789381448427 ISBN : 9789350570555 ISBN : 9789350570548

ISBN : 9789357940856 ISBN : 9789357940849 ISBN : 9789357941334 ISBN : 9789357941341 ISBN : 9789357940153 ISBN : 9789357940399 ISBN : 9789357940375 ISBN : 9789357940382 ISBN : 9789357941358 ISBN : 978935794132

FICTION/FUN & FACT, TALES & STORIES/LEISURE READING

ISBN : 9788192079660 ISBN : 9788192079677 ISBN : 9789381588659 ISBN : 9789381588840 ISBN : 9789381588857 ISBN : 9789381588871 ISBN : 9789381588888 ISBN : 9789381384336 ISBN : 9789381448069

ISBN : 9789381448090 ISBN : 9789381448083 ISBN : 9789381384343 ISBN : 9789381448076 ISBN : 9789381448809 ISBN : 9789381448885 ISBN : 9789350571248 ISBN : 9789350570210 ISBN : 9789381384329

ISBN : 9789381448229 ISBN : 9789381448236 ISBN : 9789350570227 ISBN : 9789381588697 ISBN : 9788192079608 ISBN : 9789350571644 ISBN : 9789381588734 ISBN : 9789350570180 ISBN : 9789381448168

ISBN : 9789381588314 ISBN : 9789381588260 ISBN : 9788192079691 ISBN : 9789381588291 ISBN : 9789381588956 ISBN : 9789350570852 ISBN : 9789350570906 ISBN : 9789350570838 ISBN : 9789350570883

ISBN : 9789350570845 ISBN : 9789350570890 ISBN : 9789350570869 ISBN : 9789350570913 ISBN : 9789350570821 ISBN : 9783950570876 ISBN : 9789350570920 ISBN : 9789350570937

ISBN : 9789381588987 ISBN : 9789350570005 ISBN : 9789350570012 ISBN : 9789350570029 ISBN : 9789381588994 ISBN : 9789350570036 ISBN : 9789350570043 ISBN : 9789350570050 ISBN : 9789381588406 ISBN : 9789350571552

ISBN : 9789381448182 ISBN : 9789381448199 ISBN : 9789381448144 ISBN : 9789381384404 ISBN : 9789381588451 ISBN : 9789381588581 ISBN : 9789381588529 ISBN : 9789381448137 ISBN : 9789381448106 ISBN : 9789381588178

ISBN : 9789381448175 ISBN : 9789381448113 ISBN : 9789381448120 ISBN : 9789381448151 ISBN : 9789381384701 ISBN : 9789381384718 ISBN : 9789381384862 ISBN : 9788192079615 ISBN : 9789381384015 ISBN : 9789381588185

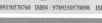

ISBN : 9789350570760 ISBN : 9789350570098 ISBN : 9789350571699 ISBN : 9789350571125 ISBN : 9789357940146 ISBN : 9789357940139 ISBN : 9789350571620 ISBN : 9789350571118 ISBN : 9789350570982 ISBN : 9789350571835

HEALTH & BEAUTY CARE/FAMILY & RELATIONS/LIFESTYLE

ISBN : 9789350570463 ISBN : 9789381588482 ISBN : 9789381448724 ISBN : 9789381448762 ISBN : 9789381448823 ISBN : 9789381384961 ISBN : 9789381384442 ISBN : 9789381448496 ISBN : 9789381588918

ISBN : 9788122307511 ISBN : 9789381448502 ISBN : 9789381384633 ISBN : 9789381448489 ISBN : 9789381384251 ISBN : 9789350570593 ISBN : 9789381384831 ISBN : 9789381384800 ISBN : 9789350570616

ISBN : 9789381384220 ISBN : 9789381384817 ISBN : 9789381384572 ISBN : 9789381448694 ISBN : 9789381384824 ISBN : 9789381384565 ISBN : 9789381384909 ISBN : 9789350570609 ISBN : 9789381448663

ISBN : 9789381448458 ISBN : 9789381384589 ISBN : 9788192079653 ISBN : 9789381384978 ISBN : 9789381448472 ISBN : 9789381448731 ISBN : 9789350571897 ISBN : 9789381448434 ISBN : 9789381448465

ISBN : 9789381448244 ISBN : 9789381384237 ISBN : 9789381384626 ISBN : 9789381448519 ISBN : 9789381384619 ISBN : 9789381448892 ISBN : 9789381384602 ISBN : 9789381588369 ISBN : 9789381588376

ISBN : 9789381588383 ISBN : 9789381588390 ISBN : 9789381448557 ISBN : 9789381588826 ISBN : 9789381384268 ISBN : 9788122305159 ISBN : 9789381448748 ISBN : 9789381384992 ISBN : 9789381384664

ISBN : 9789381448700 ISBN : 9789381588758 ISBN : 9789381384923 ISBN : 9789350570104 ISBN : 9789381448618 ISBN : 9789381448441 ISBN : 9789381384688 ISBN : 9789381384282 ISBN : 9788122308808

ISBN : 9789381448854 ISBN : 9789381384046 ISBN : 9789381384275 ISBN : 9789381384985 ISBN : 9789381448601 ISBN : 9789381448861 ISBN : 9789381384640 ISBN : 9789381384848 ISBN : 9789381384657

ISBN : 9788122310924 ISBN : 9789357940078 ISBN 9789350570357 ISBN : 9789350571200 ISBN : 9789350570340 ISBN : 9789350570944 ISBN : 9789350570951 ISBN : 9789350571309 ISBN : 9789350571828 ISBN : 9789350571781